Crook

An Anthology of New Crime and Thriller Writing

Crooked Holster

This collection © Crooked Holster, December 2016
Each story © the individual author

The Servant Problem by Finola Scott (p28) previously published in issue 1 of *The Poet's Republic* (May 2015)

Pagan by Stephen Watt (p89) previously published in *Optograms* (Wild Word Press, 2016)

Editing & typesetting: Jo Young, Sandra Kohls
Cover photography: Jo Young, Shanna L. Maxwell; SparkyInk photography
Cover design: Brenda Engberts Kaya

The moral rights of the authors have been asserted

Contents

Foreword *Andrew Taylor.*	2
See No Evil *Christopher P. Mooney*	5
Mahogany *David McVey*	11
The Understudy *Olga Dermott-Bond*	16
And We Are Hiding Now *Natalie Crick*	18
In the Gloaming *Angie Spoto*	20
The Servant Problem *Finola Scott*	28
Jackson Pollock *Cailean McBride*	29
Kit Kat *Susan McLeod*	39
Who Killed Felix? *Maggie Powell*	51
Her Father Said *Georgi Gill*	54
For the Record *Georgi Gill*	55
Anatomy of a Betrayal *Kurt Newton*	56
Raw Deal *Tom Leins*	60
Molly *Steve Roy*	71
Harmonious Music and the Spawn *Michelle Ann King*	80
New Dawn Fades *Paul D. Brazill*	83
Archmime *Stephen Watt*	88
Pagan *Stephen Watt*	89
No Place to Rest *Lucy Rutherford*	90
Newspaper Noir *Anderson Ryle*	96
A Sandwich Can't Stop a Bullet *M.E. Purfield*	102
The Long Soak *Sandra Kohls*	113
Are Ye Askin'? *Mairi Murphy*	125
Bibliographies	127

Crooked Holster

Treachery

FOREWORD

Mystery? Noir? Detective story? Police Procedural? Psychological thriller?

In the last thirty years or so crime writing in the British Isles has undergone a renaissance. It has thrown off the constrictions of the past and experimented widely. Crime writing is always about telling a story, about making the reader want to turn the page, but now we can tell that story in almost any way we want.

One reason for this is the fact that crime writers are no longer confined to authors who are published by a handful of mainstream commercial publishers. For this we must thank the growth of creative writing courses and the many publishing opportunities offered in various forms by the internet. As a result, a far larger pool of authors than ever before can see their work in print, whether on the page or on the screen. It has made it easier than ever to experiment with the genre, and to explore the many possibilities it offers.

Crime fiction is many things, but somewhere at the heart of any workable definition of the genre is this: it is about the art of surprise. In many of the best stories, perhaps their authors surprise themselves as well as their readers.

One of the many pleasures of reading the third Crooked Holster anthology is the fact that you never know what you will find next - except that it will come as a surprise, bringing with it the dividend of the unexpected, a sensation that is located somewhere on the sliding scale between shock and pleasure. The theme that links these stories is treachery, a fruitful subject for authors of all types since the Bible. It's older than Judas - and more recent than yesterday's headlines.

As you read this collection, there is a wonderful sense that everything is up for grabs. The stories constantly subvert the reader's expectations. There's a wide variety of settings and slants, crimes and corpses. If an author wants to write in the form of a poem or make a story turn on a visual puzzle - well, why not? Some of the pieces here made me laugh out loud, others chilled me, but all of them entertained me.

Taken as a whole, the anthology left me feeling full of hope for the future of the genre. On the evidence here, crime writing is in good hands, which is good news for both authors and readers. And now read on…

Andrew Taylor
2016

See No Evil

Christopher P. Mooney

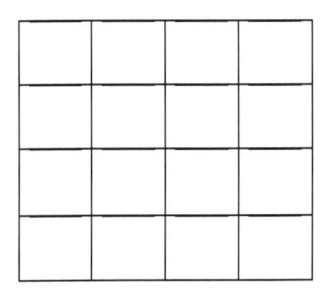

'I'm telling you there are twenty-six!' was the first thing I heard the barman say as I settled onto a stool. I'd missed my train by a matter of seconds and the pub, with its promise of warmth, seemed the only reasonable alternative to waiting on the platform for an hour.

'You're wrong on this one, Charlie,' the man on the stool nearest to mine said. He was wearing a grey coat and his face showed the beginning of a salt-and-pepper beard. 'There's only twenty-three.'

'I'm not wrong,' the barman said. 'I'm dead right. Hold on.' Turning to me, 'What'll you have?'

'A bottle of beer,' I said, not looking at him directly but over his right shoulder toward the row of fridges under the gantry. 'Something Italian.'

He turned round, took out a bottle, then turned

back to face me. 'This okay?'

I recognised the green bottle and its red-and-blue label.

'Sure.'

He put it down in front of me and expertly twisted off the cap without having to use an opener. I started in on the drink, taking a long pull.

'I don't see where you get twenty-six from,' the man in the coat said, 'I really don't.'

'Listen, Arnold, you say one number and I say another. Why don't we let this stranger decide?' the barman suggested, indicating me with the index finger of his right hand.

'Fair enough,' Arnold said, pushing a piece of paper under my nose. On it, etched neatly in pencil, was one large square containing four rows and four columns of equal-sized smaller squares. 'Look here,' Arnold continued, 'how many squares do you see?'

'Count them slowly, a couple of times,' Charlie said, 'then let us know how many you think there are.'

There was only one other person in the bar. An enormous lump of a man with square shoulders beneath a concrete face. If he stood up, he would probably be able to see the paper from there, I thought, but I couldn't be sure.

'Why not ask him?' I asked. 'All I want's a quiet drink.'

The two friends exchanged a glance but said

nothing.

I looked more closely at the paper. I counted once. Twice. Again.

'There are twenty-six squares,' I said.

'I told you,' Charlie said. 'Twenty-six.'

'The fuck there is,' Arnold said. 'Count 'em again.'

'No,' I said, more forcefully than I'd intended. 'I counted three times and each time it came to twenty-six.

'You fuckin' guys,' Arnold said. 'Just 'cause I'm the only one sayin' twenty-three don't mean I'm not right.'

'There are two of us who think twenty-six,' I said, 'and you think twenty-three. Why not ask the other guy?' I said again, nodding my head in the direction of the enormous man sitting by himself in the corner booth. 'If he says twenty-six, that makes three of us that think that way, so chances are it's right. If he says twenty-three, we can have a go at it together.'

Another glance passed between them. Then the barman spoke, his voice low, 'We're not asking him. If we ask him, he'll say he can't see nothing. He'll say he's blind.'

'Oh, I'm sorry,' I said, turning my head all the way around to look back over at the booth and noticing the white cane for the first time. 'I didn't realise your friend is blind.'

'He isn't our friend,' Arnold said, 'and he sure as

shite isn't blind.'

'I don't understand,' I said, not wanting to find trouble but curious in spite of myself. 'Maybe I should finish my drink and get moving. I do have a train to catch.' I took another big hit, looking for the bottom of the bottle.

Nobody said anything for a full minute.

Then, although I knew I shouldn't, I said, almost in a whisper, 'Fine, I'll bite. Tell me how come you think he's not blind.'

'We *know* he's not blind,' Arnold said. 'He's only pretendin' so's he can stay this side of the big door.'

'How do you mean?' I persisted.

Charlie said, 'That man's wife was murdered a couple of years back. Her cries alerted the neighbours, who called the police. The first cop at the house found her body in the marital bed. Her throat had been slit and her body was full of holes.'

'Jesus Christ,' I said, 'that's awful.'

'A fucking tragedy is what it was,' Arnold said. His voice was low but still I felt uncomfortable. I cursed myself again for having missed the train.

Charlie continued, 'That big black-hearted bastard over there was found lying on the floor downstairs, rubbing at his eyes. The cop, he put the bracelets on him right quick and brought him down the station. He said he'd been surprised by an intruder who hit him over the head. When he came to, he said, he couldn't see anything but could hear his wife screaming upstairs.'

'And?' I asked.

'And the fucking jury bought the lot,' Arnold said. 'He killed his wife, pocketed the insurance, and has been walking around with that fucking cane ever since.'

'That's an incredible story,' I said.

'But he isn't foolin' me,' Arnold said. 'I'm just waitin' for him to slip up so he'll get what's comin' to him.'

'You really think he can see?' I asked.

'Sure he can,' Arnold said. 'And if we ask him, he'll say he don't know how many squares are on this piece of paper 'cause he can't see the piece of paper.'

'You're as blind as he is, Arnold, if you think there are twenty-three.'

'That's exactly right. He's as blind as me. Which is not blind at all.'

Then Charlie again, to me, 'That'll be three quid for the beer.'

I put away the dregs then fished four singles out of my wallet and put them on the bar. 'Three for the beer and one for the story,' I said.

'Much obliged,' Charlie said.

Arnold snorted.

As I was putting my wallet back in my pocket, ready to leave, the big man got up in stages. Then, with the cane out in front of him, he walked past the length of the bar toward the street. I'll swear until my dying day that, half-way to the door, with his back to Charlie, the barman, and Arnold, who saw only twenty-three where I saw twenty-six, he looked me square in the face and winked, mouthing one word as he did so: Thirty.

Mahogany

David McVey

Then came a shout from further back in the carriage. 'Hey, Tony - did yer say you was from Mile End way?' It was Steve.

'We both know Mile End well,' said John.

'Are yer from anywhere near Starmer's Green?' asked Steve. 'D'you know it at all?'

'Can't you two bleedin' shut it for five minutes?' snarled Tony. The carriage froze into silence. The few occupants from outwith the tour group whispered nervously. Steve and John smiled to each other. Far below, a blue lake inched larger and closer as the train rattled downhill.

'Sorry about that,' said Tony's wife to Jennifer as the group re-formed itself outside the base station, 'Tony isn't very good with heights. I expect he was a bit anxious.' Sally, of course, that was her name. Jennifer had not been this close to her before, to that rich, mahogany flesh.

After the fourth night in Lucerne, there was a leisurely morning before the group was taken by bus to Lucerne railway station for the short journey to Interlaken. In their new hotel, there was more of a settled atmosphere. Danny and Tony avoided Steve and John whenever they could and if they did encounter them when doing their tour guide dialogue, simply ignored them. And though they were still voluble, the Steve and John double act became less intrusive.

On their last full day most of the group went for a trip on the Harderbahn funicular railway. On the descent, Tony grumbled, 'Another bleedin' railway, another bleedin' mountain.'

John must have heard this as he called over, 'Bet yer can't wait ter 'ave a drink in one of the pubs down Starmer's Green way instead, eh, Tony?'

'Yer, that'd be lovely, Danny could buy us a round,' echoed Steve.

There was a hushed silence, a waiting for the explosion to come. But Danny and Tony must have bit their tongues. The moment passed.

Next day, Jennifer managed the group onto their train at Interlaken and through various changes, finally parting company with them after seeing them on to Eurostar at the Gare du Nord. Of course, there had been an emotional farewell between the Spanish couples and their mother before she went through customs. 'You be good boys,' she said amongst the hugging and kissing, 'and be nice to Steve and John before you go, they're nice lads too.'

Danny and Tony embraced their mother again and nodded. All the same, it was awkward when Steve approached and held out his hand to Danny to shake, saying, 'Look us up when you're back in London, eh, lads?' Danny and Tony did shake, but Jennifer suspected it was only to please their mother.

Tony and Danny and Pat and Sally left, ostensibly to get a taxi to the airport. They didn't make a point of saying goodbye to Jennifer individually but she couldn't help feeling they looked at her in an odd way. She went outside the station and found a quiet café. There was a lot of work to do before her next group arrived tomorrow. She was twenty minutes into the admin before she heard someone say, 'Hi, Jennifer.' She whirled round. It was Steve. John, inevitably, was with him.

'What's wrong? Has something happened? You've missed the train - where's your luggage?'

'We're not getting any train,' said Steve, in an unfamiliar calm and commanding tone. 'We've got a car here and our luggage is in that. Can we have a word?'

Steve and John sat down at Jennifer's table.

'Jennifer,' said John, quietly, 'do you know anything about the Starmer's Green Bank Robbery of 2007?'

'The what? Me? No! Nothing. Well, apart from it being on the news, of course, but...'

'We think Tony and Danny know quite a bit about it,' said Steve. 'When the Met heard they were leaving the Costa del Crime to go on holiday with their old mum, they decided to dig out a couple of excoppers to shadow them, rattle their cage a bit, see if they let anything slip.'

'You're policemen? Are you brothers, then?'

'Ex-policemen,' said John, 'but no, not brothers, and we're not that bloody annoying either. That's just a little act we used to do at police socials. We've both knocked around rail and coach tours of Europe with the wives, so we were the obvious choices. Especially since we both retired before Tony and Danny were active.'

It was bewildering to hear them talk in such long sentences, and then to stop talking.

'We thought we'd better apologise,' said Steve, 'and also ask that if there's anything you remember them saying, anything that comes back to you...' he slipped her a card with contact details on it.

Jennifer stayed overnight at her usual Paris hotel and had her clothes laundered and repacked. Next day she was back at the Gare du Nord, standing by her luggage with WONDERS OF SWITZERLAND BY RAIL in large bold type on her iPad, ready to hold aloft. As she waited at the Eurostar gate, she turned, just for a quick look round. There, sitting outside a café with drinks, were Tony and Danny. They should be back in Spain by now. There was no sign of the wives. Both men were looking at her.

There was an announcement over the public address - the incoming Eurostar service from St

Pancras was delayed. She put her hand in her jacket pocket and felt the sharp corners of the card John had given her. Tony and Danny still sat, still watched her. She turned away from them, suddenly very keen to meet her new tour group.

The Understudy

Olga Dermott-Bond

Since the day of the first rehearsal, her heart had been set at a strange rake. She had watched Demetrius bouncing on his heels, ready to pounce on his lines in case they might elope into the forest without him. Without her.

Her insides were rabbit only, twitching, impaled on a slow-turning skewer of silent hope.

Opening night nerves.

The ceiling in the maths classroom was the colour of too-chewed gum. Oberon was applying snazaroo clumsily, holding his breath. Titania taking selfies. Springing up like a meadow were socks, shoes, bags – unruly, unclaimed. Stale hairspray hung like plastic, competing with naked feet. Haribo packets, the scent of what she imagined love–in–idleness to be.

She had been ready for two hours. Miss said the fairies with no speaking parts just had to have black tops and their hair tied back. It had taken Lysander so long to learn his lines that they had only had two proper goes on the stage for the roundel.

She allowed herself to glance towards the dress she would wear, hanging forlornly violet, on the back of the classroom door.

No-one had noticed yet - but soon - she knew Miss would have to ask her to take on Helena's role. Grinding up the GlycoLax had been tedious, but worth it.
She practised her favourite line to slow her shuddering, scrambling pulse – Breathe in -

'I have found Demetrius, like a jewel, mine own and not mine own…'

Better.

Her copy of the play fell open like an offering.

'The story will be changed.'

No longer the aphelion loneliness.

Itchy green carpet gulped two shades darker, and she smiled as wild thyme and musk roses sprang open at her feet, as if in love with her.

And We Are Hiding Now

Natalie Crick

For some time they sat in the cornfield
and spoke like dull mice
about what would be done.
when the sun, a ruined fruit

ripped the dilute garden growth
and spread a red alarm over tall shears
the eldest was heard to say
Bury them in the cellar.

Skins of lice lamented
over the pulsing stalks,
their drones blanched in the air
curdled and hot.

The house was distant and brown
weeping a creeping shadow from within,
that seemed to warn: Keep Out
a blaze from the forgotten.

Old plastic swing swung over the perimeter,
a goodbye, flinch.

The sky was high and blue.
In the giant shoots
lurking softly and surreal,
two ducklings on the gilded shore.

The sea was swimming with flushed young men
severing feathered heads
with long silver scissors.
pointed thorns in a paper box.

The woman roared like the man.
Stop said the girls
with frilled socks.
Once the heavens were purple

like a bruise, the corn
grew cold and wet.
The house stood waiting, a deadened bulb.
With a swift march

they advanced through the field,
cutting stems.

In the Gloaming

Angie Spoto

You might ask me what I was doing, loitering in a dark Glasgow alley at midnight. I was trying to light a cigarette, but the wind kept whipping back my flame. I stood hunched, finger flicking desperately across the lighter, the lighter click click clicking in kind. The story of how I got to the alley – the long and tiresome story of a pointless love affair – isn't the story worth telling. The story you really ought to hear is the one that begins after I finally lit that cigarette.

The cigarette smoke and the Autumn fog mingled like new lovers. I leaned back and watched the dancing of the white amorphous stuff, stark against the dark sky. It was a sound – a quick schink and snap – that caused me to look into the alley. A slim little fox was caught in a trap by its forepaw. It wasn't flailing about like you'd expect any wild animal would. With wide eyes, it moaned and licked the blood that spiked its orange fur.

A figure appeared at the opposite end of the alley. Someone who must have been hiding in the shadows. Not sure what spooked me more – the lament of the fox or the appearance of the black-clad figure – but I stepped out of sight. Whoever it was wore black gloves. Their hood was pulled up tight, and I couldn't see their face.

The figure bent on one knee, pulled something from their belt, and plunged it into the moaning creature's chest. I wish I'd looked away in that moment, that I didn't see what came next: the deft, precise movements of the figure as they sawed the fox's head off, shook it to rid it of excess blood, and dropped it into a duffle bag.

When I saw the bright blood splatter against the alley wall, my stomach heaved. I doubled over and began retching up my dinner. I must have looked like a drunk, and the figure stepped past me, paying me no mind. She – and I was certain now that it was a she – was walking down the street, totally innocuous. Call it a morbid curiosity, but I needed to know why she'd taken that fox's head. I pulled myself to my feet and set off after her.

That night became a blur of snapping traps, of crying animals, of the squelch their bodies made when she plunged the knife into their flesh. Foxes mostly, but sometimes squirrels and rats and even a housecat. A dark sort of curiosity took over, and I became desensitised to the grotesque affair quite quickly. You see, she didn't always take their heads. Sometimes a hind leg, sometimes a forepaw, sometimes just an eye. It wasn't until almost four in the morning, with her duffle near to bursting and her rucksack bulging with the collected traps, that this mysterious killer returned home. Of course, I followed her.

She lived in a dingy basement flat of a monster of a tenement building – one of those old sandstone beasts that are so common in this city. Because I kept my distance, as I had all night, I thought I'd lost her when she entered the building, but then a light flickered on in the basement flat nearest the kerb.

I swung myself over the low railing and dropped as soundlessly as I could down into the small, dark space before the basement windows. They were grimy, and they shown like frosted glass nightlights. I managed to rub a slim section clean with the end of my sleeve and pressed my eye against the glass. Sure enough, my hunter was inside. Her hood was pushed back, revealing long white hair pulled roughly into a ponytail. She now wore a dark apron embroidered in red flowers around the edges. She was far older than I expected. Old enough to be my grandmother.

In fact, the small room looked like a grandmother's house. Embroidered pillows rested plump against an armchair in the corner. A black cast iron pot squatted on an old gas stove to one side of the room, where an ancient wood furnace pressed snugly against the stove and the wall. A table, full of knots, stood in the room's centre, and a vase of flowers rested on it. On the walls hung amateur paintings of children. Must be her grandchildren, I thought, before I realized it was the same child. The same grey-eyed, fawn-haired androgynous child who smiled from every frame. The woman must have painted each one herself. In every painting, something was off, as is often the case in amateur portraits: a lazy eye in one, a crooked lip in another, a too-long nose, a drooping chin.

My musings of the paintings didn't last long. The woman dropped the duffle onto the table, slid a big rose-coloured wooden cutting board near it, and began pulling out the animal parts. I understood pretty quickly why the cutting board was pink. She'd slap a body part onto the board, cut away any excess entrails, and set it neatly aside. Some she extracted and immediately rejected, plopping them into a bin at her feet. By now, the sky was lightening. The air was the hazy green of early morning. I shot a look over my shoulder. Soon the business people would start to emerge from their houses, steaming coffee gripped in one hand, heads bent over their phones. I returned to the window. I had to know what the woman was up to, and I was close, I was sure of it.

The woman yanked a lamp closer to the table, so a yellow glow illuminated the pile of tiny body parts. And then she pulled up a chair, slid a sewing box from beneath her feet, clasped a needle between her teeth, and tugged a long, white suturing thread from the box. The rising sun was palpable now. I was conscious of it, like a blanket thrown over my shoulders. But I couldn't tear myself away from the window. The woman tugged a paw from the pile, and then the body of the cat, and she began to sew.

God, I thought, and I lurched away from the window. My fingers scrabbled for the windowsill as my foot slipped on a slick pile of leaves. At that moment, I saw the woman look up. And her grey gaze caught mine.

I clambered for the railing, slipping on wet leaves and slamming my knee into the wall. I supressed a yelp as I pulled myself up and dragged my body over the railing and onto the pavement. I crouched and scrambled out of the way. It wasn't until I was safely down the block with the sun now truly risen did the blood stop beating in my ears. It was morning. I'd spent all night following a murderous old lady as she killed and mutilated Glasgow's wildlife. And then she'd sewn them together, like a cross-species Frankenstein's monster. It seemed surreal now that the sun was up. It seemed insane.

Once home, I collapsed on the living room couch. I dozed off, but my dreams were filled with the screams of dying animals and the small, flitting spectral figure who killed them. It was the child in the paintings, peering at me from over its shoulder, from between a fuzzy halo of brown hair. Face always imperfect. Always unfinished.

When I started awake, I didn't bother attempting sleep again. I slipped out of my flat and back into the October air. I had no plan or purpose. I found myself restlessly walking Glasgow's streets, waiting for the sun to set. The mystery of the woman haunted me. I had to know why she'd done it. Why kill all those animals?

Perhaps she was an artist, working on some kind of wacky contemporary art project. Or perhaps she was a physician, and this was an under-the-table way to test a cancer-fighting drug. These thoughts flashed through my mind, but, ultimately, I didn't care for any far-fetched theories. I wanted to know the truth, no matter how morbid it might be.

'Pardon me,' said a woman's voice, and cold fingers caught my wrist. 'Do you have the time, dear?'

I was shaken from my musings, and I stopped dead in my tracks. The old woman who looked up at me smiled, her teeth glinting in the afternoon sun. I choked on my own heart.

'The time?' she asked again.

She was the woman from the basement. Up close, I could see the rivulets of her wrinkles, the small bitter nose, the pink painted lips. She apparently didn't recognize me. Maybe she hadn't seen me at the window afterall.

'Ah, almost half one,' I said after glancing at my phone.

'Yes,' she said and pulled me closer to her, the sharp points of her nails digging into my wrist. 'You have beautiful eyes.' She smiled. 'Beautiful grey eyes.'

'Thanks,' I said, pulling away.

She motioned up to the sky. 'Enjoy the sunshine. It never lasts long.'

I stepped back and watched her walk away. She was just a little old lady. A sweet old lady. But my skin burned where she'd touched me, and I felt a dark unease in my chest. I thought of following her, despite my forebodings, but reasoned against it. Not at this hour. Not during the day. But I wasn't giving up. I would find her again, and I would learn the truth.

When the gloaming finally settled over Glasgow's rooftops, I returned to the alley where it all began. All night I wandered from alley to alley, searching for the woman. Sometimes I'd think I'd hear a trap snapping closed or the shriek of a dying animal, but when I'd turn the corner, no one was there. It wasn't until half past two, that I heard the cry of a creature in a nearby alley.

I slinked slowly forwards, peering at the ground as a trail of objects came into view. A discarded boot. A pile of wet newspapers. A sleeping bag, deflated and empty. Then, standing there with her back to me, a figure, the woman. Something dangling from her hand. A lumpy mass at her feet.

Not just a lumpy mass. A man. The body of a man. His scalp was cut off and his brown, wispy hair fluttered in the breeze, hanging from her gloved grasp.

Something dark and small slinked from behind the

woman's legs. The Frankenstein's creature that had only last night been a bag of body parts. The head of a fox, the body of a cat, the tail long and thin like two rats' tails sew together. I realized something in that instant, and the idea was clear and bright in my mind: the animals had simply been practice. A prototype.

I ran in haste out of the alley. My voice caught when I tried to scream. I had to tell someone. I had to find the police. I turned down the dark road and took a sudden left and then – schink – hot pain spiked across my ankle, sending a shudder along my shinbone, forcing me to my knees.

My mind whirred. Why? Why? The sewn-together creature, brought to life by some unthinkable magic. The bloody scalp of the homeless man. The fawn hair. The imperfect paintings of the little child, smiling, smiling. And my eyes. My grey eyes. So like the child's.

You might ask me what I was doing, loitering in a dark Glasgow alley at midnight. But you won't, will you? It's not stories you seek.

The Servant Problem

Finola Scott

Wit a bloody scream! Did yi see his face?
Purple! I thoucht he wis gonnae explode!
Wit a kerryoan oer a wee drap
o' bevy that's gaen missin.
Sure that's nothing. Yi'd think
he'd loast thi crown jewels
insteed o' a few bottles o' wine.
Aye n naebudy's safe. Yi shud have
heard thi Maister oan at his missus.
Wit a laff – she's thi ony one who's supposed tae hae
thi cellar keys.
       Mind you,
               it's a pure insult.
Aw thon fuss cos he thinks we're helping
oorsels. Aye blames thi servants so
he does. It's no joke but.
Ah git scunnered when ah think
o whit his boy's up tae.
We aw ken whit he's helping himself tae.
It's thon bonny wee maid that should be under lock n
key. But of course that's no
thi same tae him. Well, Ah'll be damn glad
tae see thi back o him.

Aye Ah'm gien up the servant life
.. thi locksmiths taken me oan
seems Ah've goat a talent fir it.

Jackson Pollock

Cailean McBride

'Heads up, mate. It's your missus.'

Ray squinted through the darkness to where an unmarked Holden was pulling up to the edge of the crime scene. Through the flashing red and blues of the patrol cars already there, he could see her through the windscreen. Putting her game face on. Strapping on her gun. Slinging the lanyard with her badge around her neck. Now walking across the scrub towards them.

'What's the situation?'

Very abrupt. No eye contact. Clearly setting the ground rules. I'm not here as your wife, mate, but as your senior investigating officer. But anyone else would have at least started off with some kind pleasantry, thought Ray. It was typical of Bronwyn to go too much the other way, create a tension where none needed to exist. It didn't bother him any, but he felt embarrassed for Larry, shuffling his feet awkwardly beside him.

He pointed towards the crumpled remains of the Toyota at the end of a long skidmark on the highway, safely barricaded off behind the tape and the warning lights. Not that they were strictly needed. No rubberneckers out here. Just the three of them. And the poor bastards on the hood, or what was left of them.

'Got another Jackson Pollock.'

Bronwyn looked towards the Toyota. It was a bad smash, the car little more than a crumpled ball, the roof twisted, half shorn off and hanging at a crazy angle. But it was what lay across the car's dented and pocked hood that really caught the attention. Two people, or what was left of them, a man and a woman, draped across it, staring out at the highway with sightless, grinning horror. The key word was *draped*. Because this was no freak result of the accident. Their bodies had been dragged from the wreckage and arranged across the hood, manipulated into this pose, which, Ray mused, could have been a whole lot worse. At least they weren't made to look like they were fucking or anything. Just sitting there like a bored couple in front of the TV. No, the worst thing, he reckoned, was the bloody garland of the couple's entrails that had placed around the smashed windscreen, and threaded with little blinking garden centre fairy lights.

'Bastard even brought his own battery for those things,' he said, flashing his torch beam in illustration.

Bronwyn's face was set and grim. 'How long?'

'Not long. Couple of hours maybe. ME's on his way. Take him a while to get out here though. Surprised you made it out so fast.'

'Anything from the flash-and-cashes?'

Ray exchanged a look with Larry. He'd only been

seconded out to highway for a couple of months but he'd already found out that camera coverage out on this stretch was sporadic at best and what there was tended to be poorly maintained. It wasn't unusual to find a cam that had gone crook months previously or had run out of recording space, with no one getting around to sorting it.

'We're checking but I wouldn't hold your breath.'

Bronwyn ducked under the tape to take a closer look at the bodies. 'You got IDs?'

'James and Samantha Hughes,' he read from his notebook. 'Out of Newcastle. Heading back from visiting their folks out in Kurra. We're informing them now.'

'No kids?'

'No, no kids. Thank Christ.'

'Any sign of disturbance?'

'Take a look. What do you think?'

Bronwyn gave him a look that he knew all too well. 'You know what I mean.'

'He didn't have a root with them, if that's what you're getting at. Just dragged them out and laid them up like that.'

'And no one saw anything? No witnesses?'

'It's a quiet stretch. Chances are there's been nothing else along this way for hours.'

'Well, something bloody hit them. They didn't get smashed up like this all on their own.'

'Maybe a roo spooked them. It happens." He

pointed his torch towards the crumpled remains of the road sign at the side of the asphalt. "Sent them into that post there.'

'Sure it happens,' said Bronwyn. 'But not four bloody times in a row it doesn't.'

Ray didn't say anything. She was right, but it was irritating that she was being so pissy with them. What the hell were they supposed to do?

'Am I to take it, detective,"'said Larry, finally speaking for the first time, 'that your lot are assuming responsibility for this incident?' There was an element of hope to his tone. This was a bloody freakish mess and Highway would be glad to be shot of it.

'You take it right. As of now, this is a homicide investigation.'

'So, it *is* a homicide, you reckon?'

'Yeah,' said Bronwyn, not taking her eyes off the black empty road running horizontal to their parking beams. 'Don't you think so?'

'Sure I wouldn't know. I'm just a grunt, ain't I? You're the bigshot murder police.'

'Not that you're bitter or anything.'

'No, I'm really not.' This was the truth and they both knew it. He and Bronny had met when they were both going through training together, stuck together ever since. But she had ascended inexorably up the ranks while he'd stayed firmly in uniform. This was partly because she had a deep talent for the job, as well as a good head for departmental politics, and partly because he had little inclination to move too far from the streets, instead moving from division to division, being driven more by caprice than out of any career plan. He would have had no one to blame for his own lack of progression but himself, if he had in fact given a damn.

'The bloke's targeting crashes in the middle of bloody nowhere,' said Bronwyn. 'How's he finding them? He ain't just coming across them.'

'Maybe he has a police scanner or something.'

Bronwyn shook her head. 'He needs time to pull the shit he's doing. He can't do that if he's got HP chasing up his arse.'

'So, he's lying in wait? Driving poor bastards off the road?'

Bronwyn produced a tablet and fired it up. She swiped through images of grotesquely arranged corpses, in poses not unlike the ones they'd seen on the Pacific Highway just a few nights before.

'He's sticking them up on social media. Different accounts but traffic driven by the same hashtags. He's not put this week's up yet but it's only a matter of time. This is like some bloody art project to him.'

'But doesn't this mean you can trace him?'

'No. Different IP addresses each time. He's clearly using public terminals and the like or has a stash of different laptops and phones, or is just running some really smart software. Our best bet is to catch him in the act, I reckon.'

'Which is why we're out here?'

'Pretty much. I'm hoping we might get lucky.'

'Been a bloody long time since I got lucky in a parked car.'

Bronwyn ignored the jibe and instead brought up another screen on the tablet, showing a marked map of the rough area in which they were parked.

'The blue circles are the crash scenes, the red ones rough triangulations of where the images were uploaded.'

Ray looked at the map. 'I'm beginning to see what you're getting at.'

'Exactly. He's not travelling far. Which makes sense in a way because the less time he spends on the road, the less chance he has of us nabbing him. But at the same time, it also means he's given us less of a geographical area to cover.'

'Unless he's smarter than that and he just has everything set up here as his hunting ground and he's coming in from somewhere else to do it.'

'It's possible but doesn't alter the parameters of the search.'

'So, you been canvasing the local area? See if there's any likely candidates?'

'Of course. But nothing yet.'

'What about the universities? See if there's any creepazoids on the art programs?'

'On that too. But nothing there either. Either that or they're all too bloody weird for us to tell the difference. No, I reckon we're going to have to do this the old-fashioned way.'

'Which is why you're sitting in a candy car with me in the middle of bloody nowhere?'

'Pretty much.'

'But you're quite the bigshot down in Sydney, ain't you? You could just put some grunt on this, couldn't you? Wait for them to phone it in?'

Bronwyn coiled her arm through his. 'Who says I didn't also want to spend some quality time with my hubby?'

Ray smiled. 'Not that I don't appreciate the sentiment, but I don't buy that I'm afraid. No, there's something else going on here too.'

She looked at him. 'How do you reckon?'

'Well, you've had that look for a while,' he began.

'And what look would that be?'

'That "treading water" look. You've been a shift commander in Homicide, for what, two years and now I reckon you're getting a bit bored.'

'Trust me, Homicide is far from boring.'

'No, I'm betting it ain't. But you could be chasing Jack the Ripper and Ivan Milat all rolled into one and you'd still be looking for the next thing. That's just who you are, babe.'

She raised an eyebrow at him. 'And you think this is the next thing?'

'It's close enough. It's been weird enough to attract the attention of the media, which means it's also got the attention of the bosses. You put the cuffs on this guy then that gets you noticed. Maybe enough for you to be able to step up.'

'I'm shocked that you think so little of me,' she said, smiling.

'Oh, I think the world of you, babe. You know that. But I also know what you're like. You're a good 'tec, a great one even. Certainly better than I'd ever be.'

'That's not true. You could walk into Homicide tomorrow. Or Vice. Or any damn department. And they'd be lucky to have you.'

He smiled at the familiarity of the argument. 'Be that as it may. But this ain't about me. This is about you being happier surrounded by the suits than with the people.' He saw her mouth open to protest and so he continued hurriedly. 'That ain't a criticism, babe. That's just how it is.'

'What does it matter? If we get the bastard in cuffs?'

'I guess it doesn't at that.'

They did get their break. A couple of nights later a Highway Patrolman called Dexter Kontos put in a direct call to Bronwyn and Ray, as by now word had got out that they were the go-to guys on this particular internet nutcase. They found him on the highway just north of Newcastle, parked on the shoulder with a beat-up, white Lexus.

'What you got?' said Bronwyn, bounding from the car. Ray could see she was already buzzing with the promise of a collar. Or maybe she just had a hunch. Her hunches were usually good.

Kontos was young. He couldn't be that much older than when he and Bronny had first started on the job, thought Ray. He still had that jittery nervousness about the eyes but a few years of the craziness he'd see on the NSW highways would soon knock that out of him. But right now, Bronny was spooking him slightly, her reputation no doubt preceding her. Ray couldn't really blame him. He sometimes felt the same way and he'd been married to her for 11 years.

Kontos pointed to the Lexus. 'Found her here. Lights off, just sitting in the dark. Thought there was something crook about it so I thought I'd take a look-see.'

'And what'd you get?' asked Bronwyn.

Kontos flashed his torch along the side of the Lexus. There were a series of dents and deep scores and scratches, as well as evidence of maybe two or three different types of paint etched within them. It also looked as if an amateurish attempt had been made to clean up the car, knock out the dents, scrub out the paint, but it had only been half successful.

'Christ, she's been in the wars, ain't she?' said Ray.

'Where's the driver?' asked Bronwyn.

Kontos nodded towards the driver's door. 'In there. Meek as a bloody lamb.'

The driver was a 29-year-old called Alwyn Wilson, a BVA drop-out with badly henna-ed hair, a faceful of piercings and a history of mental health issues. Forensics matched the paint on her Lexus to each of the crime scenes and she went down, in a blaze of publicity, for 20 years. It was Bronwyn's name on the arrest sheet, and in the papers, with Dexter Kontos barely getting a mention. But that would be OK. Bronwyn always remembered her friends.

And Ray, he was happy too, pleased for Bronwyn as she stepped up to the division commander spot, and no longer so antsy and tetchy in their day-to-day. Besides, the boost in dollars would be come in handy. There were, aside from Wilson's victims, no losers here.

Kit Kat

Susan McLeod

Kate checks her watch. Thirty minutes now. Long time to be kept waiting. She should be at the hospital; he'll be out of theatre soon. Instead, she's stuck in a tiny room with blank walls, blank floors, blank ceiling.

Just a few questions about the incident, Mrs Truman. Time is critical if we want to catch the assailant. That's what they told her.

What do they want to know? She goes over yesterday in her head and fits the pieces together.

Hands move, fidgeting with hair, necklace, paper cup. Long-cold tea slops onto the table and she hunts in her handbag for a tissue. Finds her vaper and thinks of stealing a puff or two. Turn the dial up and hide in a cloud of smoke. Not the same as a fag though. Not as good as a drag on an Embassy No.1. She'd hold the smoke inside until the nicotine hit her brain. Two years since quitting and her fingers are still yellowed. Those stains will never fade; they'll always be with her. Like stretch marks. She thinks of her son.

Where is Aiden? In London by now, surely. But he has friends down there, knows how to disappear. Will need to, if he did as she told him.

A scuff from behind the door. She does not look. Refuses to give the satisfaction, just lets the seconds bleed away.

The station was busy when she arrived, lots of familiar faces helping with enquiries. Ronnie's brother was amongst them. He'd looked impassive – face like putty – but pale. No sleep, just like her. She'd wanted to spit at him.

The door opens and two men come into the room. They look impossibly young.

'D.S. Swann.' He is bulky in his suit with a hairless head. Like a giant baby. He sits opposite. 'Thanks for coming in, Mrs Truman, this must be difficult for you.' But he smiles as he speaks and the words are empty.

'D.I. Lake.' A taller man, also in a suit, but lean. He positions his chair to the right as if umpiring a tennis match. Busies himself with a file.

Two detectives. Baby and Umpire. Kate doesn't recognise them – they aren't local, must have been brought down from Manchester - and a spasm of fear grips her. What do they see across the table? A middle-aged woman, dumpy in an over-sized tee shirt and wash-greyed sweatpants, dirty hair tied back in a ponytail. She folds her arms and squashes her breasts flat. What do you expect, she wants to scream, after the night I've had? A fucking blow dry and manicure? She can't read their expressions; they are blank.

'What are you doing to catch the bastard? The one who tried to kill my husband?' If in doubt, attack. She is the victim, after all. Remember that.

'We just have some things to clear up about the attack last night.' Baby is casual.

'What things? Someone broke into our home and …'

'I know, I know. Please bear with us.' And he smiles again.

The temperature in the room climbs. Sweat trickles down her back. Baby's cologne irritates her nose. She longs for her vaper. Longs to blow smoke in his stupid grinning face.

'This attack seems to be connected to a recent spate of drug-related incidents.'

She stops thinking about his aftershave. 'Drugs?'

'Mmm. A new supply hit town in the last month. Black tar, they call it. Clogs your veins. Eventually, your flesh dies. Grim.'

She allows her mouth to hang open. 'That's awful … '

'It's triggered a turf war. Your husband may have been caught up in it.'

'Terry's got nothing to do with drugs.'

'Wrong time, wrong place, Mrs Truman. Could happen to anyone. He goes into the wrong pub and bumps into the wrong people.'

She flinches. Tries to remain calm as Baby babbles on about bad luck and bad eggs and other nonsense, hoping he hasn't noticed.

'Why did your husband go to the Bearded Duck

last night?' This is Umpire. 'A hipster pub full of reclaimed church pews, surf board tables and artisan lagers. Terry's at least twenty years older than the clientele. Why that pub?'

The pause is tiny, almost imperceptible. Once she begins to speak the words jostle to come out, to compensate for the hiatus.

'Yeah, Terry went there. Just for a pint, you know, after work. He fancied a game of pool. Best tables in town, he always says. I wouldn't know, don't know one end of a cue from the other.' A self-deprecating smile. Silly old bird, what could I know?

'He found Ronnie Deysher there. Sitting cool as you like, selling skag to kids. Wrapped it in sweet wrappers so it looked straight, yeah? Well, Terry went mental, proper mad. Punched Ronnie in the face, told him to take his filth elsewhere.' She stops, looks at the table. 'At least that's what Terry told me when he came home. In a right state, he was. Had to clean him up a bit, stuck a bag of frozen peas on his jaw.' Now she looks up, stares Baby in the face. 'But he was in the right. Scum like Ronnie Deysher shouldn't be on the streets.'

'When did Terry become such an upstanding citizen?' Baby seems sceptical. 'He's got a record for possession. Breaking and entering.'

'Hash? That's not real drugs. Don't count.' Shakes her head. 'Sides, we lost a niece to smack. Lisa. Lisa Macken.' She blinks. 'Last year ago. Drugs ruined her. Terry's never forgot.' She freezes for a moment, loses her train of thought and goes somewhere else. Remembers a blue-white face.

'What about the breaking and entering?' Baby prompts her.

'That was over ten years ago. Terry's got his own business now, is a respected builder.'

'And what happened to the skag, Mrs Truman?' Umpire breaks in, softly.

'What do you mean?'

'From the Bearded Duck pool room. All that sweetie-wrapped heroin. Where did it disappear to?' He cocks his head to the right and affects a puzzled expression.

'Dunno.' She frowns and looks away, past Baby towards the door. 'I wasn't there, remember.'

'Of course,' Umpire agrees. 'But, you've recreated the scene so vividly, I wondered if you could help us with that little detail. Maybe one of Ronnie's associates took the merchandise. Whilst your Terry was being a social crusader.'

She feels his eyes crawl over her face like maggots. 'S'pose. Like I said, I weren't there.' And shrugs.

Umpire leans back and seems to lose interest, nods at his colleague.

'Let's move on to later yesterday evening.' Baby takes over.

Terry had phoned just after five. Gave his laughing assurances that he would only drop in for a quick pint, get the lay of the land.

'Aiden's meeting me there.'

'Be careful, Terry.' She was urgent, suddenly mindful of her son. The Bearded Duck was alien territory.

'No worries. I'll be back before nine.' And he rang off before she could reply.

It was past eleven when they finally blew into the living room, laughing and joke-punching each other. She could tell something had happened. When Aiden headed off upstairs straightaway, she was sure.

'Well?'

Terry threw himself into the armchair. 'You won't believe it. Look at that.' He handed her a red-wrapped chocolate bar, a Kit Kat. 'What do you think it is?'

She could tell it wasn't genuine from the feel of it, the weight of it in her palm.

'Smack, that's what.' He told her about finding Ronnie Deysher selling the Kit Kats in the pub, how he'd laughed when Terry walked into the pool room. Deysher didn't laugh for long though. 'I punched him, kicked him out into the street. He caught me a good one too.' He touched his jaw, prodded at the blooming bruise, and smiled. 'Swore he'd sort me out, that next time I wouldn't be so lucky.'

'You're too old for this, Terry.' She was unsympathetic. 'You know where the frozen peas are.'

Then he dropped the bombshell. 'And Aiden grabbed the gear. It's all out there in the hall. Must be about twenty grand worth.'

She shouted at him. Screamed. How he could bring that rubbish in their home. How he could involve their son in all this. After everything that had happened. After Lisa.

'Ronnie Deysher is bad, through and through. He killed Lisa. Dangerous."

'Katie, Katie – they were taking the mick. Dealing in plain sight. I couldn't just walk away, you know that.'

'Whatever. Get it out this house tomorrow. You're a real fuckwit sometimes, Terry.' Her parting shot ricocheted; Terry was bullet-proofed by victory.

A noise woke her in the night, a sound from below. The digital display on the alarm clock said one thirty. Must be next door's cat, messing around in the extension again. She nudged Terry.

'Sort it out.'

He stumbled off, grumbling.

The alarm clock clicked onto one forty-five and he hadn't returned. Eventually, she crept downstairs, switching lights on as she went.

Light from the kitchen exposed the scene. The half-built extension was a mess. Plastic sheeting flapped in the gaps left for windows. She saw naked legs kicking against the brick floor. A figure sat on

Terry's chest. Terry's kicks were weak, spasmodic. He was dying.

She picked up a cement-flecked radio and hit the attacker. He dropped beside Terry and made a gurgling sound so she hit him again, just to be sure. White clay covered Terry's eyes, ears, nose, mouth and an empty Polyfilla gun lay next to his head. He'd boasted of only buying the best, not those cheap brands. She pulled his lips apart and clawed at the putty but it filled his mouth and throat. He was suffocating.

She grabbed a Stanley knife from under the overturned worktable in the half-built extension. Held Terry's head back and cut a vertical slit in his windpipe, just under the Adam's apple.

Pulled the straw from a discarded McDonalds drink cup. Jabbed the tube into Terry's neck and breathed into it, once, twice.

Waited.

Breathed into the straw once more.

Felt air puff against her cheek. Felt the rise and fall of his chest as he inhaled and exhaled. Felt sweet relief. It was like giving birth. She made the necessary calls. Got Aiden out of bed. Started to clean up.

Kate stared at the man in the back of the van. A blood meandered down his forehead onto the metal floor. He must have split his head when she knocked him out. The ambulance was on its way, would be here soon.

'Can you hear me, Ronnie?' He stared up at her. Every eyelash studded proud of those wide eyes.

'Can you feel that lump filling your mouth?' He nodded, cheeks bulging as his tongue moved. Gaffer tape covered his mouth and fastened his ankles and wrists together.

'That's one of your Kit Kats. One of the sweets you were selling in the pub. Swallowing is a reflex action – just stroke the throat until it goes. I got three down your throat before you woke up.' His eyes rolled.

'Do you know why your punters inject smack?' She waited for him to shake his head before continuing. 'Because that's how they get the rush. The euphoria.'

Lisa had told her that. One of their pointless conversations that ended with Lisa promising to try and give up and Kate believing her. Neither of them meaning a word. Knowing it was bollocks. Lisa always went back to Ronnie and always went back to smack.

'If you eat it... well, not so much of a hit. Too gentle for a junkie.' Ronnie wriggled, tried to break the tape binding his limbs.

'The amount you've swallowed, if you're lucky it won't be long before you slip into a coma.' He groaned. 'If you're lucky that is. That black tar H though is filth, full of crap. You might stroke, convulse, drown in your own blood.' She took a deep breath.

'Nobody trespasses into my home, Ronnie. And nobody hurts my family. Not ever. You should have stayed in Leek with your brother.' She smelled hot piss. Felt nothing.

She remembered the last visit to the bedsit Lisa had shared with Ronnie. What she found there.

'I could make it all go away.' She lifted the nail gun and rested it on his forehead. He stared, white encircling his irises. She saw Lisa lying on the carpet again, dirty spoon beside her, needle in her vein. Vomit-stained cheek. Blue-cold. The colour of death.

'You promised never again. No second chances.' She slammed the van doors shut. Slapped the roof and watched the lights disappear down the lane. Aiden would dump the body and catch the first train to London. Get some distance between him and this mess. Redesmere Water was a lovely spot. Deep too. Ronnie won't reappear until Spring.

A siren from the front of the house interrupted her thoughts. The ambulance was here. She prepared a face to meet the other faces. Is this how actors feel before stepping on stage?

Kate returned to the house.

'How did you know how to do that?' Umpire stares at her, incredulously.

'What?'

'The throat thing. You saved his life.' Umpire asks.

She sniffs. 'Saw it on telly once.'

Now Baby is laughing; he slaps the table. 'No way. With a Stanley knife?' She stares at him, a level gaze that holds tight until he stops gurning.

'Did you see who attacked your husband?' Umpire asks.

She shakes her head. 'No. A figure running away … that's all.'

'Are you sure?' Umpire asks. 'See we think we know who attempted to murder Terry. We think Ronnie Deysher wanted revenge because Terry humiliated him in the Bearded Duck. And now Ronnie has gone missing.' He leans forward. 'Your statement could help put him away. Is there any chance it was Ronnie you saw running away?'

'I'm sorry … I was in a right state. Wasn't thinking straight. Terrified.' She looks at Baby with pleading eyes.

'Surely, you want the man to be punished? If you identify him, you'll be doing the right thing by your family. You'll get justice.' Baby asks.

'Justice?' she repeats dully. 'Don't know what that means.'

Umpire waves his hand in front of his neck, game over, let's wind this up. They work through the formalities, thank her, send regards to Terry, but their hearts aren't in it, Kate can tell. She's wasted their time.

Baby opens the door for her and guides her out. All the interview room doors are closed and voices cough away inside, telling lies and spinning evasions. Ronnie's brother is in one of the rooms – she hopes he is as confused as his interrogators, hopes that he is worried about his little brother. Kate shuffles away down the corridor, clutching her handbag. Time to go back to the hospital and see Terry.

Time to confess.

Who Killed Felix?

Maggie Powell

There was a body, and unless Felix had perfected the art of slitting his own throat, with hands tied behind his back, there had been a murder. Gently slumped, nothing to tell of a death struggle. Only the silent, open mouthed wound, where a silk necktie should be, rust red stains seeping into cream axminster, and black stockings strangling his wrists. Closer inspection at the Post Mortem, indicated that being tied up was not a new feature in Felix's life.

This was news to his grieving trophy wife, or so she said. She had a cast iron alibi, as solid as the hospital plaster going on her arm at time zero. She had 'fallen' at home earlier that evening.

SOCO teams found nothing to hang a case on. All of his colleagues, family and ex-wives were alibied to the hilt. None of this, 'I was watching telly on my own' rubbish. Being first on the scene, I was prime suspect for all of ten minutes, until they checked out that I was being filmed for a TV interview, during the six and three quarter minutes it took him to bleed to death.

I organised the funeral. I had taken care of Felix for decades. Anticipating his every whim, I watched out for that look on his face when he grew bored with someone, and eased their way out of his life, before it became a crisis.

Then one day I caught that same look...a half smile. A lucky glance in a mirror. That smirk, gone before I turned round again, had been aimed at me. Treachery!

'Felix my dear,' I said, 'May I take a couple of days off for a personal project?'

'Of course Mother, Sophie will fill in for you.'

He already had a replacement, but what was the plan? I knew all of his passwords. He had arranged the *curator bonis* documents, and my exile was to be in a remote care facility, presumably with permission to dope me into docility.

I made plans too. Booked the children, their mothers, and significant

employees into an isolated, all expenses paid resort, to celebrate 50 years of trading, or some such blah. Getting a first time freebie from Felix, they didn't ask questions. I offered a 'tell all' interview to a hungry journalist. Final touch; I provoked a 'domestic' to get harmless Trophy out of the way.

It's still an unsolved murder, but life goes on. Trophy took her share of the estate and drove off to happiness with the Chauffeur, my grandchildren had their Trust Funds topped up, no chains attached. Debts were paid, business sold off, accounts settled. Just one payment to make in cash...untraceable notes. Left in a Tesco bag for life...you don't need to know where.

Survival is a cut throat business…and the contractor was a lot more exuberant than I had expected her to be! I needed to survive, but not in a living death.

The prime mover in Felix's retirement was Felix himself.

Her Father Said

Georgi Gill

Her father said, 'I will go out in the streets,
find your attacker, beat the living daylights out of him
for touching my
daughter. I need my shoes and my big coat.
Mind you, it's dark out, late now. He'll be long gone
– best call
the police –

though the police won't take you seriously.
They'll claim you're the one to blame, say you led
him on. It's your word against his
- I know how this will go, I've seen it all
on telly. The police are all wrong for this. They won't
understand

you, not like I do. You are the victim here.
It's not your fault but it is dark out, and why did you
walk down the alley
alone? Of course you didn't ask for it
but – well – no one smart paddles if there's crocodiles
in
the river.

Her father counselled her, 'I wouldn't tell your
mother if I were you. I mean, you're fine. You're not
seriously hurt. Right,
it's not that bad. Don't tell your mother. You'll
only worry her. We don't want that. It's best if you
keep quiet.'

For the Record

Georgi Gill

The story of my life does not exist.
Does not exist. Ask away - I'll refuse.
Try lay me bare as a fat Titian nude.
My tight lips won't slip even when I'm pissed.
I mask silence in noisy artifice,
a politician burying bad news.
Bastard bloodhound, you will exhume dead clues;
I chew my bloody tongue but you persist,
call silence my close-fisted accomplice.
We stare each other down like blind statues
and I admit I'm tempted to give the gist
to you. Just you. Alone. But then I'd lose
it all and, when boredom dictates, you'd twist
the rules, leaving me detached and dismissed.

Anatomy of a Betrayal – A Five Part Dissection

Kurt Newton

1. *Through A Wide-Eyed Flense*
I apologize for the delay. Today's subject: a forty year-old adult male. Cause of death: blunt trauma to the head. As you can see, the subject's skin is clean and unblemished, a clear sign of health and fitness. The device I am holding is called a dermatome. It is a useful tool for harvesting large areas of surface skin. Let us proceed.

What's that? Yes, it does appear that the subject's eyes are moving, dancing in their sockets as if experiencing a pain so excruciating it is like none he has ever experienced. But there is no cause for alarm. It is a normal autonomic reaction. I assure you this man is dead.

What's that, again? Dr. Garner? Yes, this man does indeed resemble my good friend and colleague, Dr. Garner, who couldn't join us today due to a prior engagement. No more interruptions, please.

2. *A Pound Of Flesh, And Then Some*
Now that the skin has been removed, we can see the well-defined musculature beneath. A simple incision here and there and we can remove large portions of

body mass without interrupting blood flow.

Excuse me? Of course, you are correct, there shouldn't be any blood flow. This cadaver, however, has been kept in a carbon dioxide bath since death. Although temporary, it does provide the illusion of bodily function.

Yes, I do see that the eyes are still moving. Yes, it is unusual for such reactions to continue. Yes, I have heard of such a drug that when injected will induce a paralytic state where the patient will exhibit little if no outward reaction to the most intense pain imaginable, a method purportedly used by some third world dictatorships to torture unruly dissidents. Now, please, I ask all of you to hold comment until after this particular procedure is complete.

3. *Disorganization*

Now on any large-scale removal process it is important to retain blood flow. Notice the intricate network of veins, arteries and lymphatics that sheaths the body much like a fishnet stocking. Like the kind my wife wears when she's feeling horny. But my work comes first—she knew that when she married me. If she was feeling lonely, she could have read a book. She didn't have to—

I'm sorry, where was I? Of course: the organs. It is amazing how many the human body can do without. One lung, one kidney, yards and yards of intestines. Even as major organs are removed, as I am demonstrating here, the body as a whole will continue to survive, redirecting its energies toward more vital functions such as the brain and the heart. But like marriage and best friendships, even those will begin to falter and fail in time. So I must work in haste. I mean, let us move on to the next topic.

4. *Weeding The Bone Garden*
We are now down to the framework, the wire figure upon which each of our bodies is formed. If this subject were still aware, these neural branches, which I have preserved so meticulously, would still be responding as if attached, spasming ghost muscles with the slightest touch, inducing wave after wave of pure agony.

As you can see, this bone saw makes quick work of the extremities. No more racket ball for you, Phil. No more creeping into my home at night and crawling into bed with my beloved wife, Marsha. One. Two. Three. Four. You'll dance the night away no more.

What did I say about the interruptions? Yes, I am aware I called the cadaver by name. And, yes, I do realize that Phil is also the first name of my colleague and good friend, Dr. Garner. And many of you have probably seen the picture of my wife, Marsha, on the desk in my office. So?

If this were Phil, and he were indeed guilty of an adulterous act with the woman to which I was faithfully, matrimoniously bound, and he were conscious, as has been suggested by one of our students, wouldn't he deserve it? Wouldn't they both?

5. *Postmortem*

In closing, I would like to apologize for my digressions. It is highly unprofessional of me to mix professional responsibilities with matters of the heart. A cold and uncaring heart, as I've been told. As dead, perhaps, as the one upon this table.

But there I go again. Now, I hope you have all been paying attention, those of you still here. I hope I didn't work too quickly. And for those who stayed, I trust it has been educational.

It is really too bad that some of you left, for I have decided to extend today's lecture. After a brief intermission I will return with our second subject of the day: a thirty-six year-old female that will bear a striking resemblance to my wife, Marsha. Pure coincidence, I assure you.

Raw Deal

Tom Leins

Albert Erasmus gestures vaguely over his stooped shoulder at the prowl car. It is moving at kerb-crawler pace down Palace Avenue, and the fat plainclothes cop in the passenger seat glares at us.

'You know what they call a Paignton cop in a three-piece suit?'

I shrug, already bored of his shtick. Already bored of his face.

'The defendant.' I stifle a yawn. He chuckles and wheezes.

His expensive clothes hang apologetically from his scrawny body. His lesions are becoming harder to conceal the more rampant the illness becomes. His hair is still as black as tar, but his eyes are opaque, like contraceptive jelly. His third marriage disintegrated last year, and he is currently living with a much younger man in a welfare hotel.

He fumbles at the latch on his crocodile skin briefcase with crooked fingers. It is empty except for a videotape.

'Ready to have some fun, young man?'

Back at his rented office space, Albert slots the videotape into the top-loader. I'm old enough to remember when this guy was still a big deal. He was the town's preeminent defence lawyer. He was into shit so deep that you could stir it with a stick. He drifted between clients – worked with the Italians, the Poles, even the Albanians once or twice. I have heard stories about him playing his paymasters off against one another, and his downward career trajectory wasn't a surprise to anyone.

Even so, his decline in stature makes me feel uncomfortable, but then again, I've seen some of his peers beaten to death with pipes or thrown off multi-storey car parks for similar transgressions, so he has something to be thankful for. A few bad choices – a few bad clients – and you are flushed down through the system like a greasy turd. You end up in shit creek – or splattered across Palace Avenue – whichever comes first.

Albert presses play on the unit.

His partner, Peter Kovacs takes up the whole screen. He is smoking and sipping tea. He is a good guy – one of the best. He scraped Erasmus off the ground and offered him a leg-up when he hit rock-bottom. He got me off the hook after a little misunderstanding with a hand grenade and a glue factory a few years ago. He quit the defence game not long after, and now he works in land law. I guess he has his reasons.

Kovacs clears his throat.

'If you are watching this video, it means I am dead.'

Dead? I'm temporarily dumbstruck.

Then the camera zooms out, slowly. The viewfinder

is shaking, like the cameraman is trembling.

Kovacs offers a brief, grim smile and then his skull-meat is splattered across the lens. The triggerman then turns his attentions towards the cameraman. There is a quick yelp and then the sound of a couple of bullets thudding into flesh. The camera crashes to the ground, and a bejewelled hand slumps in front of the lens. A pair of spit-shined boots stomp across the linoleum and tread on the hand. Then a black-gloved hand reaches down and switches off the camcorder.

Before I realise what is happening, I am out of my seat, and I have Erasmus up against the filing cabinet by his scrawny neck. I feel myself squeezing the life out of him.

'You rotten bastard…'

I see the look of unadulterated horror in his eyes and drop him to the floor.

'Who?"

He is gasping, crying milky-looking tears.

'I swear to you, I didn't know what was on the tape, son…. I was offered a grand to play it for you.'

'Who?'

'I never met him in person. He made contact over the telephone.'

'Tell me everything you know, Erasmus, or I swear I will snap your fucking neck.' My hands are shaking too much to snap matchstick right now. Luckily he scares easy.

When I arrive at Paignton police station later that afternoon, two elderly cops are taking turns to hose down the holding cells. They ignore me, and continue smoking and talking amongst themselves. I trail soapy footprints down the corridor towards Carver's office.

He's sitting in his swivel chair wearing a cheap open-throated sports shirt and brown slacks, his big feet resting on the desk. Despite his casual attire I notice that he is still wearing wingtip shoes. The lines etched on his hangdog face look deeper than ever today. His eyes are so red they look diseased. He is intently watching a portable black and white TV.

'Busy morning?'

He shrugs.

'Average. One streetwalker. Beaten to death with a brick. At least she wasn't dumped in Paignton Harbour this time. Those girls swell up like you wouldn't believe.'

He laughs unpleasantly, then yawns.

'Well spit it out. I'm technically on holiday – as of this morning.'

Francis Fazakerley. What do you know about him?'

'Businessman. Husband. Philanthropist… Scumbag. Implicated in at least three murders in the last five years. You don't accumulate a property empire like his, in a town like this, without a few bold gestures.'

I grunt.

'You know Peter Kovacs?'

He nods. 'The lawyer, right? Straight shooter?'

'He's dead.'

Carver sits up sharply.

'That's news to me. You got a body?'

I shake my head.

'There's a video. An execution. Kovacs and some other unfortunate. Very bloody. His partner – Albert Erasmus – told me that he was working for Fazakerley on some kind of land deal. Helping to grease the wheels with a guy named Hollis. Some kind of big-hitter at the Department of Water and Power...'

Carver holds up a hand to stop me, and twists the volume knob on the TV.

Fazakerley is onscreen. He was aging badly the last time I saw him, and that was two years ago. He is wearing a hard hat. I take a step closer to the television. He is sweating so hard it looks like he is melting.

He is up at Paignton Yards, surrounded by local dignitaries. I recognise the ravaged asphalt sprawl in the background all too well.

'Ladies and gentlemen, the problem with this town is that there is no money, but plenty of potential. Too many housing developments have stalled due to hollow promises about funding. We have been spoon-fed greasy, unpalatable lies by unscrupulous holding companies time and time again. I am here to get this investment back of track. My fellow investors and I have reached our target of £5 million, and plan to break ground as early as next month. Make no mistake, to succeed we need to learn the lessons of the past, in order to pave the way for a brighter future.'

Carver switches off the television and laughs, mockingly.

'Greasy, unpalatable lies? Sounds about right. Here are my files on Fazakerley. Your name pops up once or twice, but then again, you already knew that, didn't you?'

He slides a manila folder across the desk towards me.

'Look after yourself, pal.'

He swings his feet off the desk and leaves the office, whistling a show-tune. I hear his wingtip shoes echo down the corridor as he leaves the building.

The humid August heat is exhausting. The sun-blurred asphalt positively shimmers in front of me. I'm sweating by the time I arrive at the Department of Water and Power building. I follow the plastic laminated signs in search of the planning department. The entire sub-section seems to consist of one portakabin.

The secretary looks faded and slightly yellow, like an old photograph. She is piling her possessions into a cardboard box. A cigarette dangles from her heavily lipsticked lips. Smoke curls lazily up to the ceiling.

'Excuse me, Miss...?'

'Call me Sylvia, darling.'

Her thin fingers work another cigarette from the pack, even though she's only halfway through the current one.

'What can I do for you?'

'I would like to speak to Mr Hollis, if possible.'

'Oh, darling! Harry is retired. He finished last Friday.'

I scratch at my stubbled jaw and check my note pad.

'Retired? He was only 47.'

'It's alright for some, isn't it?" she giggles

'Do you have any contact details? A forwarding address, perhaps?'

'Harry kept himself to himself. We weren't close.'

'Wife? Kids?'

'Oh no, Harry wasn't the marrying kind.' She gestures to a photograph of him with the mayor. He is wearing more jewellery than Liberace.

'I was hoping to enquire about an application I filed recently... do you have access to his files?' She looks me up and down, curiously.

'Well, not to be indiscreet, but that is something of a sore point.' She gestures over her shoulder to a four plastic bin-bags. 'He had a funny turn on Thursday. Accidentally shredded a few of the wrong documents.'

'A few?'

She smiles sheepishly. 'The rest of the bags are outside.'

Fazakerley mostly works from home, but he keeps an office on Palace Avenue for important meetings. It is opposite the premises that Kovacs and Erasmus operate out of. How do you like that for a coincidence?

The security guard at his building is called Ormond. He used to work as a hammer boy for Remy Cornish, back when that was still a valid career option. The older I get, the more I realise that this town is full of mercenaries. Leftover soldiers from old, messy wars. When the dust settles everyone still wants a pay-day, and they don't care how they get it.

Ormond flashes me a mirthless smile and buzzes me through.

Fazakerley's paisley tie has been loosened, and he is wielding a putter. His ball hits the lip of the expensive cut-glass tumbler and skids across the shag-pile into the skirting board.

'Mr Rey! Long time, no see. What can I do for you?' I shake his hand. It feels warm and fleshy.

'I'm looking into the disappearance of Peter Kovacs. I have been informed that you hired him to broker some kind of land deal, up at Paignton Yards.'

'Disappearance? That is unfortunate. Nice man. Thorough worker. Good hourly rate.' He frowns, unconvincingly. 'How about a drink?' I nod. The best thing about undertaking jobs for wealthy men is usually the drinks cabinet. He scoops the tumbler off the carpet and polishes it on his sweaty-looking shirt. 'Scotch?'

'Two fingers, one cube of ice.' I nod.

He smiles, appreciatively. 'So, Mr Rey, tell me more about our mutual friend Mr Kovacs…'

Later. The Dirty Lemon. Ormond is drinking at the bar, still wearing his navy blue security guard uniform.

'Drink?' He gulps down the remainder of his pint and nudges his empty glass towards Spacey Tracey.

I rack my brain for small talk, but it never was my strong-point, so I drink in silence instead.

'How's your uncle?"

He grunts.

'Why don't you dig him up and ask him?' The memory hits me like brass knuckles.

Three years ago it was rumoured that Francis Fazakerley had buried two contractors under a new-build in Foxhole. One of them was supposedly Ormond's uncle. Fazakerley denied all knowledge of the burial, and the killings were pinned on a mutual acquaintance named Sullivan Price. I leave my half-drunk drink on the bar and drift towards the door.

'Hey. Where are you going?'

I ignore him and head down town towards the taxi rank. I slide into the back seat of the first cab I see. It is unlicensed, but I don't mind. It is what people have taken to referring to as a 'voodoo taxi'.

'Where to, my friend?'

'Paignton Yards.'

'£10 surcharge this time of night,' he grunts. It's not even 7 o'clock.

'Sure. Whatever. Say, do you have a shovel I can borrow?'

'No, but I have a pick-axe in the boot.'

Man, this fucking town…

Moretti's Ristorante is a poor-quality facsimile of a cliche. I half expect to see shiny-suited Mafioso shit-bags sipping plum brandy and fiddling with their shoulder holsters.

I drift through the restaurant like a blood-splattered ghost. The man opposite Francis Fazakerley is so fat he looks incapacitated. His steak is bloodier than my shirt. Seriously, who goes to an Italian restaurant and orders steak?!

'… and I said to him, I'll take heaven for the climate, but hell for the company!'

The fat man's laughter ricochets off the bare brick walls.

A waiter tries to intercept me, grabbing me by the elbow, but I shrug him off, slamming my elbow into the bridge of his nose. It gives way with a wet crack.

I feel bad for him. Violence is rarely my first choice of action – it often seems to be my only choice. Fazakerley swivels in his seat, and I kick his chair away. He catches his head on the table on the way down.

Blood leaks from a gash across his receding hairline. He wipes the crimson smear out of his eyes with a napkin. His grey eyes bore into me, as he hisses under his breath:

'What the fuck do you think you're doing?'

I empty out the contents of the Tesco carrier bag on the table. A mouldy arm bone, with bejewelled ring fingers, lands on his plate. The fat man sitting opposite Fazakerley vomits into his own lap.

'You are already acquainted with Mr Hollis, Fazakerley. Where is Kovacs?'

He grunts noncommittally, so I grab him by his hair and drag him through the restaurant. He leaves a pissy smear on the carpet.

Outside, Ormond and Albert Erasmus are leaning on Albert's car. Ormond is clutching the taxi-driver's pick-axe. He grins malevolently at Fazakerley. Albert is trembling like a junkie with the jitters. He has a small pearl-handled revolver clamped in his liver-spotted hand, but can barely bring himself to look at the bleeding man at my feet.

I don't care about men like Fazakerley and his sweaty little plans for this town.

'Listen, Ormond...'

Ormond swings the pick-axe into Fazakerley's left kneecap with a sick crunch and he hits the pavement like a sack of shit. He howls like a dying dog.

I clap Albert on the shoulder as Ormond heaves Fazakerley into the gaping car boot. Then I slowly start to walk away. My work here is done.

Molly

Steve Roy

His oxygen was nearly gone. The tanks offered little now, save wisps and a memory and changing in the front seat of his Ford didn't help much either. It was a tight fit as he struggled into his pajamas and a robe, causing him to use more breath than he could spare.

George had parked beneath a river oak at the far end of the lot behind the Brook Wood Hills Assisted Living Center. He spent a lot of time at nursing homes, now that his emphysema had reached stage 4. No security to speak of and they offered an inexpensive source of oxygen and the occasional Fentanyl patch, which George used to self-medicate his sciatica. His weathered face and threadbare robe allowed him to blend in easily, though he was fifteen years younger than the average patient.

George erupted into another coughing jag as he exited his Crown Vic and by the time he was done, all he wanted was to be home, languishing in his La-Z-Boy with a Chivas in one hand and a Chesterfield in the other. Unfortunately, that would have to wait, for in addition to the oxygen and the Fentanyl, he'd come to Brook Wood for a job, a resident needed to be iced.

The vic's name was Molly Sanford, an eighty-three-year-old widow with a middle aged son and no grandkids. She lived in room 238 and apparently someone felt she'd overstayed her welcome on this old earth. George hated taking out an old broad like that, but a job was a job. He needed the air, he needed the patches and mostly, he needed the money.

His reflection from the side window of his midnight blue Ford showed everything was in order. No visible drool anywhere, check, cheesy tangerine colored pajamas, check, blue terry cloth robe, check, Dearfoam slippers, check, Oxygen cart, check.

Oh yeah, better ditch the cigarette. He took a last drag and flipped the Chesterfield, and its twenty great tobaccos, behind a nearby dumpster.

George headed inside, staring absently at his Dearfoams as he shuffled by the nurse's desk. No one looked up. He began his search at the end of the hall on the right, checking each room for the tell-tale no-smoking signs, or even better, zombified Fentanyl eyes. He found a fresh set of tanks at his third stop and switched them out for his empties while an overweight Alzheimer's patient watched without purpose.

Like picking up a new propane tank at Home Depot, he thought as the sweet hiss of fresh air filled his lungs.

Four rooms later, he peeled a fairly fresh patch from a semi-comatose Hispanic guy who smelled like he hadn't been changed in a week. George made a mental note to report Brook Wood's less than optimal hygienic conditions to the proper authorities.

Having finished his more mundane tasks, George took a moment to apply his newly purloined patch before heading up to room 238. He hoped Molly was asleep. Even though he'd been doing this kind of work for thirty years, it still bothered him when they watched. Leo said it was because deep down, George had a good heart. George wasn't so sure. Maybe he was just a pussy.

Stifling another cough and having fortified himself with a cup of lime JELL-O he'd filched from a cart in the hallway. George poked his head through the door and was pleased to hear Drew Carey asking some pinched-faced housewife about the price of tapioca pudding on 'The Price is Right'. Even though he'd liked Bob Barker's shtick better, things were setting up perfectly, the room was a single, the TV would drown out any stray moans and best of all, Molly was sleeping.

George wheeled his new tanks to the side of the bed and watched her for a moment. She was a pretty little thing, frail and drawn and her head barely dented the pile of pillows there. He'd intended to take her out right away, using one of those pillows under her head, but she looked so peaceful that he decided to wait a few moments. Besides, she hadn't touched her dinner.

George couldn't bear to waste perfectly good mashed potatoes, so he dug in as he glanced around the room. Her nightstand held three or four pill cases, none of which would do anything to ease the pain in his back, a bottle of Estee Lauder which reminded him of his own mother's bedroom and a picture of a sallow faced mook with a rapidly fading hairline, squinty eyes and no discernable chin.

The spuds were tasty enough and so was the creamed chicken. Unfortunately, halfway through his impromptu meal, Molly woke up. She looked at George without a trace of surprise and used the remote control by her hand to silence the ever perky Mr. Carey. Apparently a strange man in her room was not as upsetting as one might have imagined.

'Well, hello,' George said through a mouthful of industrial strength gravy. 'I bet your wondering why I'm eating your dinner.

'Not particularly,' Molly said. 'I don't have much of an appetite these days. Just as happy to see someone else enjoy it.'

'Well thank you, ma'am. I'll be done in a second.' George said, as he finished the last of her Le Sueur peas. He thought about scarfing down the cling peaches as well, but decided against it because peaches sometime gave him the winds.

'My name is George.' He extended his big meaty hand which enveloped the birdlike digits she offered.

'I'm Molly. 'It's a pleasure to meet you, George.

I'm glad you stopped by. I always enjoy company.'

George still wasn't ready, so he pointed to the picture by Molly's bed. 'That your son?'

Yes, that's my Sheldon.'

'He's a good looking kid,' George lied.

'That's kind of you to say, George, but it's not really true, is it?' she said. 'I'm afraid Sheldon takes after his late father, Harry.'

'Is that so?' George said.

'Yes it is. You see my Harry was a good man and confidentially,' she said with a sly grin, 'he was a demon in the sack, but he wasn't much of a looker.'

George smiled and he felt the tension in his back ease.

'My Sheldon's an actuary with a big insurance company in Atlanta. He lives in Peachtree City now and I don't see him too often.' Then, as if remembering some important addendum, she added. 'It's a long drive.'

George winced at the disappointed look on Molly's face, what with Peachtree City a mere twenty-five-minute trek from Brook Wood Hills.

'I guess I shouldn't complain. He's a busy man,' she said without a hint of concern. 'I'm afraid I've been a bit of a disappointment to Sheldon lately, what with my still being alive and all.'

George started to protest in politeness, but she held up a meatless hand that seemed almost translucent. 'No it's true. He never says so but I can see it in his eyes.'

George suspected Molly was right. Kids could be real assholes and after all, Sheldon was the reason George had taken this particular gig.

'I see you have some breathing challenges, George.'

'Yes ma'am. emphysema, I'm stage four, now,' George said, like the fact of his coming demise was a badge of achievement. He coughed three times in succession as if to punctuate his condition then wiped his mouth with his sleeve, glancing at his robe quickly to make sure he hadn't started bleeding again.

'Pity,' she said with a soft edged curl of her lip. He recognized in that kindly turn, one, who like his own mother, would take on another's burden if she could. 'I understand that can be quite a challenge.'

Molly sniffed softly as if catching an early spring aroma. A different smile crossed her face now, this one, more sharp edged and playful. 'You're still a smoker though, aren't you, George. Be honest with me. We always recognize our own.'

George looked down at his feet and reddened, like a kid caught with his first pack. 'I've tried ma'am. I really have. I just can't seem to give them up.'

She reached out and patted his hand and her skin felt as thin as tissue.

'That's alright, sweetie,' she said. 'I smoked two packs a day for almost fifty years. The only reason I gave it up was I couldn't get anyone to bring them back from the Kroger anymore.'

George thought about that for a moment.

'Well how'd you like one right now?' he whispered, flashing the rumpled Chesterfield pack from his robe. 'Go ahead, they'll never know.'

'You know, I think I will, since you've been kind enough to offer,' she said. 'But George.' All at once her tone grew schoolteacher stern and George's eyes widened.

'Ma'am?'

'I certainly hope you don't intend to light up with those things on,' she said, nodding toward George's oxygen tanks.

'Sorry ma'am. I do forget, sometimes.'

'That's very dangerous, dear. They can explode. You need to be more careful.'

George turned the valve off, lit the Chesterfield and placed it in Molly's mouth. She drew deeply and a look of complete contentment crossed her face. One drag seemed to release a lifetime of memories and moments.

He sat on the edge of her bed and listened to the silence as the old woman enjoyed her last smoke. The comfort of a cherished friend like Mr. Chesterfield washed the ravage of years and the fear of time from her face. And in her own space and moment, she butted the cig into the cling peaches.

'Well, I guess I'm ready, George.'

'Are you sure, ma'am?' George said, feeling surprisingly reluctant. 'It's still early.'

'No, it's actually quite late,' she corrected. She smiled one last time and this one was as different from the others, as day is from night, for it was full and rich and it showed George what she must have looked like as a young girl, pretty and strong willed and ready to meet the world. It made him wonder about her life and how she'd ended up with a shit-heel son like Sheldon. George's heart nearly broke in that moment and he casually brushed away a touch of dampness from his eye. He was just a big pussycat inside. Leo always told him that too.

'You know, Molly. You can still call this off. I won't hold it against you.'

'No, George, I'll not do that. I've had my time and a body just wears out after a while. And of course, there's Sheldon. He tells me how unhappy he is and how he wants to become a day trader, whatever that is. He tells me if he just had a large enough stake, he'd be set for life. You see, I have a tidy little nest egg saved up and I suspect Sheldon is dying to get his hands on it.'

George nodded in his most comforting way. It was always easier when they relaxed at the end.

'I need to be gone and he just doesn't have the fortitude to do it himself. You see, he's not a very strong person. He's like his father in that way as well. That's why I called you, George. You come very highly recommended.'

'Thank you, ma'am. Are you ready then?

'I believe I am. You're doing me a service. You will keep that in mind, won't you, dear?'

'Yes, ma'am. I will.'

'That's a good boy,' she said and patted his hand again. 'One last thing, George. I'm curious about this life you live. Does it make you happy?'

He thought about her question for a moment then smiled a sly and special smile of his own, despite the tears which had begun to fall freely now.

'Yeah,' he said. 'It does. I guess this is what I was meant for, the path that's best for me, you might say.'

'Well that's good then. I think everyone should be happy at what they do. I know I want Sheldon to be happy. In the end, all any of us ever want is for those we love to be happy.'

George saw the truth of her words and he nodded in agreement. He picked up one of the pillows and fluffed it in his hands.

'Goodbye, Ma'am,' he said and kissed her forehead.

'Goodbye, George. It's been nice meeting you. And remember to turn those tanks off when you smoke.'

Harmonious Music and the Spawn

Michelle Ann King

There's always been something about my sister that makes people want to give her things: sweets, drinks, tickets to clubs, lifts in shiny red cars.

Today's benefactor is called Hank, and he's given her a giant pink balloon that floats above her head, getting in the way of the other tourists' photographs. They're trying to capture Times Square and getting a lense-ful of rose-pink latex instead, but Symphony apologises sweetly and none of them complains. Something else people like to give her is the benefit of the doubt, which is often more useful than the gifts.

Hank thinks she's a singer, and that Symphony is a stage name. It's not; our parents were simply big fans of the orchestra. They also loved horror films, which is why they called me Regan, after the possessed little girl in The Exorcist. That's us: harmonious music and the spawn of the Devil. I told Hank I'm a writer, which covers a multitude of sins: cynicism, morbidity, general weirdness. People will excuse a lot if they think you're the creative sort. And they always think they'll star in one of your stories.

Hank buys us lunch and we get the subway back to his hotel. All around us, people sit with highlighters and printed-out manuscripts on their knees. Writers, editors, agents? Maybe all three. This is New York, after all — the centre of the universe for commercial creativity. I'm sure aliens always start their invasions here because they want to get on the telly.

Hank whistles as we go up the stairs to street level. He asks me some desultory questions about my opinions of the city, the other things I want to see. The hints are not subtle. Hey, here's a great idea — why don't you go do that now, Regan? I'll look after your sister.

I answer the questions he speaks aloud and ignore the others.

Symphony presses her face against a souvenir shop window, sighing over a shelf of pastel-coloured cowboy hats stamped with the ubiquitous I Heart New York slogan.

Hank buys it for her. Hank buys her everything she wants.

In his room, Symphony sprawls across the bed and opens every packet and bag at once, exclaiming with delight over cookies and crackers, pastries and pretzels. A small, flat bottle of toffee-coloured bourbon glints gold in the fading light.

Her knife, when she takes it out of her jacket pocket, glints silver.

I close the curtains and stand between Hank and the door. Finally, belatedly, he starts to look uneasy. This script is not playing out as he expected.

'Hey, what—' he says, but doesn't get any further.

It doesn't matter. I can guess what he was going to ask because it is, I think, something we'd all like to know: Who is the star of this story? Who is the hero, who is the bad guy? How is it going to end?

New Dawn Fades

Paul D. Brazill

The water looked pitch black. Or at least, a lot darker than it had seemed in Spark's dreams and memories. The harvest moon's reflection only occasionally scuffed the lake's dead surface. But it still looked tempting, inviting. Like a means of escape.

It was at times like this when Howard Spark wished he believed in something. Had a religion, maybe. He'd seen the Catholics clutching their beads and mumbling their mumbo jumbo but it had no impact on him other than creating a feeling of contempt. Scorn. Superiority. He knew that life was only a brief crack of light between two dark voids, after all. It was obvious. Only an idiot could think otherwise. Usually. But now, well ...

He hadn't been to the lake in years. The last time he'd been been a teen. That was when Morgan had killed Fowler. It was an accident, of course. Drink and dope-fuelled shenanigans from kids who were too young to hold their substances. But Fowler died just the same. And all that youthful innocence had disappeared like spit on hot pavement. Twenty-five years to the day.

He threw a stone into the water. It sank with a low thud. He remembered a song he and Leek had liked when they were kids. Something about being a pebble making ripples. Howard had thought of himself in that way for many a year. Making dirty red ripples wherever he went. Well, drips mostly. Sometimes floods of crimson. And he'd been proud of his … impact on the world. He wasn't one of those mindless, autonomous drones that dragged themselves through life making no impression on it, good nor bad. Proles. Epsilons. Victims.

But now the past was crashing into him. Pelting him with bitter memories. Battering him with guilt. Ever since the doctor told him about the cancer, his world had been slipping through his fingers like grains of sand.

He sat down against a gnarled tree and took a couple of packs of diazepam and a bottle of Grant's whisky from his raincoat pocket. He swallowed a handful of tablets and washed them down with the whisky.

Howard closed his eyes and thought about the old days. He smiled. Then the sea of sleep enfolded him.

David Fowler had made a lot of promises over the years, most of which he'd never kept. He'd promised to give up smoking. To cut down on the booze. To take up jogging. He'd promised his first wife that he'd stop shagging Cathy his secretary and made a similar promise to Cathy after he'd married her. That'd all been smoke and mirrors, of course.

But the day he'd promised to kill Howard Spark he knew it was a commitment he wouldn't back out of.

Everyone had said his dad's death was an accident but David knew who was really responsible.

He listened to Joy Division over and over again as he stood in the bedroom and prepared for the trip to the lake. He dressed in black and pushed a black balaclava into the back pocket of his jeans. He put on a Kevlar vest and took a Bowie knife and a Walther PPK pistol that he'd bought from a Polish copper that drank in his local and pushed them into a black holdall.

The reminder message on his iPhone buzzed. He looked at the message: Time To Kill. He deleted it and head downstairs. He stood in the hallway and listened to Cathy pottering in the kitchen.

'Off to my lovely night shift, Cath. See you in the morning, luv,' he shouted, and left the house.

He didn't hear her reply.

'Twat!' said Lee McAvoy, as he kicked the car, hurting his foot in the process.

He knew it was his own fault for being such a tight arse. For buying a cheap, knackered Volkswagen Touran. For doing the repairs himself and not getting a proper mechanic. For getting a second hand Sat Nav. And now the bloody car had broken down and he was stranded in the middle of nowhere. He knew it was his own fault but that didn't exactly help matters.

It was bad enough being up north but getting stranded in the boonies, stuck in the middle of nowhere … It was like a scene from Deliverance. All he could see were bloody trees. He looked at his knock-off Rolex but it was too dark to see the time.

He got back in the car and sat waiting for another vehicle to give him a list somewhere but nothing passed. It was getting cold too. He checked his flask but it was empty. He knew it would be morning soon and he'd be able to see better when dawn broke. Did the sun rise in the east or the west? He didn't know. He didn't need to know. He was from Lewisham.

He decided to get out of the car and walk around for a bit. See if he could spot any signs of civilisation. He put his parka on and headed up the road. After a while, he saw a light in the distance and decided to head toward it.

David could see Howard sitting against the tree. He could smell him, too. He stank of booze and disappointment. David felt the disgust and anger consume him. He took out his gun and slowly, silently moved closer. As he loomed over Howard, he saw that the old man was already dead.

David roared with rage.

The satisfaction of revenge had been torn from him

Lee could see light ahead. As he got closer he thought he saw a parked car. He heard what sounded like a wild animal and paused. Then there was the sound of sobbing.

Lee staggered forward and tripped.

'Oh shite,' he said as he staggered and slammed onto the man that was crouched down in front of him.

David twisted and turned, his gun held out, just as Lee banged into him. Lee fell on top of David pushing the gun barrel toward David's chin. The gun went off. Lee dragged himself off David. He staggered back, covered in blood.

'Fuck! Fuck! Fuck!' he said, and collapsed onto his back, panting.

He opened his eyes and looked above the tree tops. He saw a taste of daylight.

He dragged himself to his feet, ignoring the corpses, and headed back the way he'd come.

It was almost dawn.

Archmime

Stephen Watt

Pale-rose sunstone inside the kirk
sheens from the stained-glass windows
rendering slayed Saints;
the butchered relic of undetermined remains.

The Archmime enters
flaunting imitations, personal gestures
    the family know only too well,

        encapsulating
        those finest characteristics,
        those atypical peculiarities

    which steered towards his execution.

Behold the painted expression
of innocence, vulnerability,
arms, heart, eyes – open.
Photographs would only miss the impression,
the congenial qualities
never captured in a poem.

Police watch the performance from the rood loft
alongside the crows and stone angels,
leaving the forensics to swab
the inside of warehouse whiskey barrels,

apply blood and hair to a thespian's depiction;
    a stalker's recital.

Pagan

Stephen Watt

Jewellery trees flicker silver fruits
as a finger of moon
kindles the gloomy woods
in plated disco lights; the ashen
videotapes of childhood.

She is unlicensed.
Ribbon sleeves scatter rainbow dust
over licking flames, lusting
after oxygen and prophesised rain,
the gusts of wind cleansing flesh –

the remains of something
 smouldering afresh upon a stone.

Hands are turned upright like the antlers
crowning her head
while rain crystals dab the capillary bed
of her long tongue,
trapped like insects in a salivated cobweb.

A neon-red Mohawk
spikes from behind the nearby mountains.
She dismisses her council of librarians,
teachers and accountants
to douse the wood smoke
in urine the colour of Jerusalem thorns.

Resurrection rabbits could well dig up those bones
then some mongrel will howl for its master
who never returned.

No Place to Rest

Lucy Rutherford

It had taken Rupert and Miranda more than three years to find 'the perfect house' as she called it. She was very particular as numerous estate agents could unhappily testify. Flicking through 'Country Life' Miranda said 'It needs to be absolutely right as I don't see us ever moving again. We're too old for all that. This is the last time we'll change houses and I want this to be my final resting place, so it has to be just what we want with no compromises.'

Rupert was more pragmatic. 'For God's sake, darling we've got years ahead of us. We're only in our fifties. If we buy the big house that you want, and I get the perfect garden to grow vegetables in, there won't be much resting for either of us. Even though I thought we wanted to take life a bit easier?'

Eventually though, they did find a wisteria covered, honey coloured Somerset rectory and a lifestyle that allowed Rupert to retire early from the world of advertising and Miranda to become the lady of the manor. The young oily estate agent Justin, had successfully down-played the small graveyard that lay in the grounds. 'They'll be quiet neighbours, and the gravestones have been colonised by nature and wildlife so it is a kind of eco-system.' Rupert nodded approvingly as he mentally laid out his vegetable patch as far away as he could from the fallen stone angels and broken headstones.

Miranda would have preferred that it wasn't there, but the rest of the property and grounds ticked so many boxes that she accepted the compromise. 'It looks quite gothic and atmospheric, Rupert. And if we really hate it we can complain to the diocese and see if they can't relocate the bodies. I'm sure no one visits the graves anymore.'

Rupert relished the challenge of landscaping the large garden and creating something to nourish them both. He had a potager garden in mind – stylish and functional. He put away all his designer suits in a wardrobe in one of the bedrooms and comfortably slopped around in cords and Viyella shirts and surrounded himself with gardening books and even bought software to plan out the garden on his computer. Since Miranda and he never had or wanted children this project would be his baby, and it would be a legacy to leave to the world. A way for his name to continue.

However, as was often the case their goals were different. Miranda's agenda was to prioritise renovating and redecorating the house and she made lists of tasks for Rupert that kept him out of the garden. The list grew exponentially. Every time he settled down with his plans she would say to him 'don't forget to tick something off the 'to do' list darling.'

Whenever he attempted to venture into the garden, slipping his feet into his Wellingtons in the boot room, her voice would travel after him. 'Not too long Rupert – house first, garden second. Remember?'

The Rectory became a tyranny. The Georgian pile ate up money and time, and was fast becoming a millstone round their necks. It always needed maintenance – there was always a brass door handle that didn't turn or a sash window that needed freeing. Damp appeared under the shutters and the mouldings had cracks that showed a re-plastering job was on the cards. One evening Rupert came in after a precious hour in his sanctuary of his garden and was just then mentally installing a pergola when his reverie was shattered as he walked across the upstairs landing.

Miranda came towards him 'Darling,' she called, 'Just look at that other patch of damp. See? There, above the Gothic arch? Look Rupert at where I'm pointing, for God's sake. If you didn't spend so much time in that bloody garden you'd see where the problems are for yourself and spend some time putting things right.' She waved her arms over the balustrades of the minstrel's gallery. Rupert didn't doubt her diagnosis for a minute. Miranda was a great harbinger of doom, but he wasn't going to look. He didn't need to as he knew what he'd see. He walked briskly past her and without pausing pushed her straight over the mahogany rail with the flat of his hand in her back. He heard her land as he carried on walking towards the bathroom. 'Should have done that years ago,' he said.

He spent an untroubled evening in his study drinking whisky and planning his garden. As he raised his glass in the air it occurred to him that there was a pressing need to dispose of the body. He surveyed her lying crumpled on the floor and another large whisky provided him with an inspirational solution. He would bury her in the graveyard - who would ever suspect that?

His gardening regime rendered him fit for the task so taking a shovel and his wife wrapped in one of her numerous and pointless throws he made his way down to the cemetery. The moon helpfully emerged from behind the clouds as he selected an ancient tomb that had a stone box affair on the top. Heaving the slabs aside he dug down six foot. He enjoyed the feeling of digging so much he almost forgot the purpose of his task. He casually dropped his wife in the hole and filled it in before moving the stones back in place.

As he walked back into the house with a light step he knew his plan was brilliant. She'd rot down nicely, with no smell and no one would ever look in a graveyard for her. Next day he carried on as usual and had no thoughts for his wife until his back ached and he remembered that burying her may have caused the stiffness. Nothing that some 'Deep Heat' wouldn't put right. He cast his mind back to how easily his wife's body had gone into the hole. Why?....Because she wasn't stiff! She was still soft! Come to think of it she wasn't even cold. For God's sake – don't say she was just unconscious? Shit! She could be buried alive. He paused then shrugged. 'Oh well can't be helped she'd be dead now anyway.'

Rupert happily continued with his life, occasionally boasting to his tomatoes and petunias about the perfect murder. No one had known them well enough to realise that his wife was even missing, so he wasn't concerned when an official from the Diocese – a Mr Taylor - appeared one morning.

'I hope, Sir," he smiled, "that I am the bearer of glad tidings.'

'I'll be the judge of that,' snapped Rupert. The single male life had rendered him curmudgeonly.

Mr Taylor's polite smile continued, "The church recognises Sir, that there can be a blight on house prices caused by disused graveyards in the vicinity. The Bishop has ordered that the little cemetery adjacent to your property be moved to a corporation facility. We will grass it over after the works and you then have a choice as how to incorporate it into your lovely garden here.'

Rupert was ashen and his mouth hung open.

Mr Taylor continued, 'you really have done an amazing job with these grounds, Sir.' It looks like something from a magazine. Have you submitted it for an award? You should be jolly proud of what you've done. Whatever fertiliser you use is brilliant. I've never seen blooms that big. '

Rupert looked on glassy eyed. He didn't hear the compliments which in other circumstances would have had him smiling and explaining his plans. All he heard was 'It shouldn't take us too long to excavate and reinter the incumbents. We always have a police officer standing by – it's just the regulations you know. I can understand why your dear wife wrote to us and explained how badly the graveyard impacted on your horticultural projects. Such was her insistence on its unwelcome presence Sir, that we took her seriously, and I can really see what she means now. Is it possible to meet her and see her reaction to the good news?'

Newspaper Noir

Anderson Ryle

'What are you reading, kid? I asked.

'The paper,' he answered without looking up. His dirty brown hair hung down over his forehead and hid his eyes from view.

'I can see that. Aren't you a little young to be reading anything but the funnies?' I lit my cigarette and tucked my lighter back into my coat pocket. The kid didn't answer.

'Say, does that paper cover the Reynolds case?' I asked.

'Yes.'

'Listen, kid, I'll give you a quarter for it.'

'Go find your own newspaper,' he responded. 'There is a box on every street from here to the post office, Oak Street, Linden Street, and Magnolia. Take your pick, but leave me alone.'

'How old are you?' I asked, a little incredulous at the boy's manners.

He folded the paper and smoothed it across his lap like an old grandpa finally resigning to his grandson's incessant questions. 'I'm twelve.'

'You have a job?'

'Yeah. A paper route.'

'Shit, you run a paper route and you won't sell me

one newspaper? I just want to see the latest on the Reynolds...' the kid cut me off.

It's a messy divorce. Jim Reynolds still says that his wife stole a hundred thousand dollars worth of art from their mansion, and now she claims that he's been cheating on her. Says she even hired a private detective who found proof.'

'Kind of grim stuff for a twelve year old to follow,' I said, taking a drag on my cigarette. 'Who did she hire? Was it Bosworth? That sucker has out-maneuvered me at every turn. It's not my fault though; he's well connected.'

'Paper didn't say who she hired.'

'I've been following the case, trying to get in on the action. I'm a private eye myself. There's just one thing I don't understand. If Bosworth was hired to scrape dirt on Jim, why didn't he call to rub it in my face? There aren't many private investigators in this town; I usually would have heard if there was a big fish on the market like Sally Reynolds.'

'I don't know, mister. I'm just the paper boy.'

'Say, do you know when Sally made her statement to the reporter?'

'Not for sure. Ed Finch, who writes most of the articles on the Reynolds, told me that this case has been developing so fast he's had to talk to his sources in the morning just so that he can get his piece in by the afternoon deadline.'

'If that's true, then Sally would have had to make

that statement yesterday morning. Jim Reynolds has been out of town on business for a week.'

'Is that so?' the kid asked without interest.

'Yeah, he just got back in town late last night. I'll bet Sally Reynolds never even hired a private investigator. It's possible she hired someone from out of town, but I think she's trying to bluff him out. If she can make him nervous about losing even more in the divorce, he might settle the case and drop his theft charges. She's no dummy.'

'Doesn't matter now,' the kid said, looking westward, down the street.

'What do you mean?'

'He's dead. Jim Reynolds is dead.'

'What the hell!' I said in surprise. 'Jim Reynolds isn't dead.'

'Sure is.'

'Give me that paper,' I said, snatching it from the boy's lap. He didn't try to stop me; he just looked off down the street again like he wished that he were anywhere but there.

I read the short article where Sally claimed to have proof of her husband's infidelity. It said nothing about Jim Reynolds croaking. 'He's not dead. It doesn't say anything about Jim being dead,' I said, as I thumbed over to the obituaries. 'Where did you read that?'

'Didn't read it. I saw it.'

I put the paper down and tried to look the boy in the eye. He was staring off down that street trying his best not to look at me. There was a glistening drop of moisture precipitating at the corner of his eye, and he was fighting hard to keep his voice from shaking.

'I saw it while I was on my paper route this morning,' he continued. "You know how they have those big glass windows in their bedroom? I was about to throw the paper from my bike when I heard yelling. I've been keeping tabs on the case, so I thought if I could get close enough to see, I might learn something nobody else did. Maybe even get my name in one of Ed Finch's crime columns.' The tear couldn't stay put any longer; it rolled down his cheek, and he smeared it away with his wrist.

He heaved a deep breath and then carried on with the story. 'I walked up to the house with their paper in my hands. Saw that there was some movement in the bedroom window, so I crept over there, hidden by the bushes. I saw her, Sally Reynolds; she was laughing at him. She said that she had caught him with his pants down, and that she would get half of everything now. Then he called her a bitch and threw her on the bed, tried to strangle her. But she kept on laughing. It scared me, mister. Honest to God, that laugh scared me worse than anything I've ever seen at the horror pictures.' The boy breathed in silence for a few moments, trying to regain control.

'Go on, kid.' I said, nursing the last shreds of

nicotine from my cigarette. 'What happened next?'

'Well, he was standing over her, trying to choke her to death. And his eyes were all closed shut while he was strangling her, as if he didn't want to look at what he was doing. She was still laughing like a banshee. Finally, she reached under the pillow and pulled out a gun. Blew his head open.' The boy started crying, and his little body was heaving up and down. I put my hand on his shoulder and his sobs intensified.

'I don't want to be in Ed Finch's column. I don't.' He said between sobs. 'I just want to forget I was there.'

'You don't have to talk to any reporters,' I said. 'You don't have to do any of that. It's ok.' I kept my hand on his shoulder and pitched my cigarette into the street.

'She knew he was going to try to kill her. She was ready for it.' He said as he wiped his tears away, and started to regain his composure. 'Why would she do that? Wasn't one hundred thousand dollars' worth of art enough? Did she really have to kill him for the rest of it?' He closed his eyes and rubbed them one last time. 'She's going to tell the police it was self defense; she certainly let him put the strangle marks all over her neck. I guess I'll have to go down to the station too, make my own statement.' He looked like the most world-weary private eye I had ever seen, and he was only twelve years old.

'Kid, you'd make one hell of a detective.' I said.

'I don't know about that,' he replied. 'When I saw what happened, I froze up. Forgot to leave their newspaper on their porch; I just kept on clutching it tight in my hands, all the way back here where you found me.'

A Sandwich Can't Stop a Bullet

M.E. Purfield

Purdy stood in the hallway of the apartment building and held the large box with two hands. It was empty but he tried to make it appear like a television was inside. He hoped the apartment door would open soon. The brown UPS uniform that was so tight he felt like his intestines were going to pop.

The locks on the other side clicked and the door opened. The man in his thirties blinked as if adjusting to the light. It was almost noon. From what Glossman told him the man should have been asleep.

'Raphael Durango?; Purdy asked.

He scratched the stubble on his cheek and said, 'Si. That for me?'

Purdy shifted his weight as if he were going to drop the box soon.

'Would you like me to bring it in? It's heavy.'

'What is it?'

'I don't know, man," Purdy said. "It's from Sears. Did you order a television or stereo?'

'No. I don't think so. Unless my wife did.'

'Do you want it or not?'

'If it was a mistake do I get to keep it?' Durango asked. Purdy groaned. The box slipped through his fingers. 'Okay, man. Come on in.'

Durango held the door for Purdy who carried the empty box inside. The front room only had a couch and a large television across from it. A rack of women's clothes was close to the bare windows.

"You can just put it on the floor," Durango said.

Purdy placed the box by the couch and followed the man into the kitchen. Durango sat at a small table and picked up the sandwich on the dish. The kitchen appeared just as barren as the front room. No appliances except for the refrigerator and stove and take-out garbage on the counter.

'You just move in?' Purdy asked.

Durango held the sandwich, chewed, and nodded.

Purdy opened the tablet pouch that hung over his leg and pulled out a Maxim 9; a 9mm handgun with a built in silencer that gave the barrel a short box shape and allowed it to fit perfectly in the pouch. Durango's eyes widened. He held up his hands and the sandwich to shield his face. Purdy pulled the trigger. The first shot pierced the sandwich, punctured Durango's forehead, and burrowed into the kitchen counter. When his hands dropped to his lap, Purdy fired a second slug into the bridge of Durango's nose, which pushed the man backwards to the floor.

Purdy stared at Durango's body and sighed his boredom.

The next day, Purdy checked his box at the Five

Corners post office. Inside he found a few advertisements and small box from Orion Industries, one of Glossman's fake companies. He took everything out, dropped the mail in the garbage can, and left with the box.

He then went to the Bank of America where he requested to open one of his safety deposit boxes. As usual the woman behind the desk threw a skeptical expression at him. Purdy, at twenty-eight years old, stood six foot and weighed two hundred pounds. Most of the weight was in his stomach. His face held a few scars around his cheeks and forehead as if an army of cats attacked him, making the light blue in his eyes seem colder. He wore a brown-stained jeans and a worn black hoodie that smelled of body odor and fluids. If his face and chopped blond hair weren't so clean he could pass for homeless.

Once alone with one of his boxes, Purdy opened the small package from Orion Industries and took out the newspaper wrapped block. Underneath it was a brick of old twenties and fifties. He didn't bother counting it. Glossman was always good for the second half of the payment, not like his other regulars who soon became irregulars.

He positioned the money in the box. It fit perfectly with the millions in cash but next time he would need more space. He placed the box back in the slot, left the bank, and decided to kill some time at the library.

Purdy was eating a Philly cheese stake at Zapps! on Oakland when Binko entered. The man in his mid thirties wearing camouflage shorts and a Teen Titans Go! tank peeked around the restaurant as if he'd never been there before. Purdy shook his head and chewed. He first met Binko at Zapps! five years ago. They shared a few clients and often discussed them.

Julian, the owner behind the counter, finally caught Binko's attention and made him order some food or leave. Binko did and brought his standard slice and mozzarella sticks to Purdy's table at the front window where they could keep an eye on the cops who went in and out for their food and banter.

'Hey hey, man,' Binko said. "What's shaking?"

Purdy stared off at the construction across the street. Another abandoned warehouse/factory was slowly changing into condos for the rich.

'Nothing much,' Purdy said. "What's good with you?"

'Man, it's getting rough out there. Had the cops over at my place the other day,' Binko said. 'Yeah. No shit. But they weren't there to bust me. Someone told them that they saw me take a little boy into my place. You believe that shit. Disgusting, man.'

'They search it?'

'Hell no. With my lab all out in the kitchen and shit?'

Purdy nodded.

'Fucked up.'

'It was probably one of the old tools that complain my weed leaks out into the hall. I so gotta move.' Binko shoved two mozzarella sticks in his mouth. 'Where you been?'

'I just saw you here three days ago.'

'Yeah. But you haven't been to my place to score in two weeks.'

Purdy shrugged.

'Drying out. Moving to Mexico. Retire, you know.'

'Nice. Think your clients will give you shit?'

'I doubt anyone will complain. Maybe Glossman. He's the only one who uses me regularly.'

'You won't hear a peep from Glossman no more.'

'What you mean?'

'You haven't heard? Oh shit. Yeah.' He leaned in closer. 'Glossman's fat ass was popped last night. While the guy was making dinner someone must have snuck in or something. Took off his caps and did him a mercy in the head.'

'Cops know who did it?'

'Please, that list is as long as my dick. Glossman should have been out decades ago. Think the guy knew Moses,' Binko said. 'So when do you think you're going to leave?'

'Gonna meet a potential client tomorrow. If it seems easy, and it probably will, and if Radicci is done with my papers, I'll be gone by the end of the week.'

'Nice.'

Purdy sat on the bench at Pershing Field Park. He sipped an iced soda he bought at the pizza place across the street on Central. For the next twenty minutes he gazed off at the kids playing on the renovated jungle gyms that the city took too long to build. Parents chased the younger ones around, trying to keep them close while the older kids cursed, talked tough, and failed to impress.

A woman in her mid twenties sat down next to him. She wore gray pants and a blue top. Her straight long dark hair framed a tan face with blue eyes. She crossed her thin legs and watched the kids play.

'How long have you been a cop?' Purdy asked.

'I'm not a cop,' she said.

'Lawyer? Work in any capacity with the law enforcement?'

'No. I work in an accounting firm in the city.'

Purdy knew all that. He had her checked out before the meeting.

'What can I do for you, Ms. Patel?'

'Three months ago my younger sister was raped. She's seventeen. At first she wasn't going to do it, but I convinced her to press charges. She identified him in a line-up. He was arrested and brought to trial. She sat in front of the court and relived her story to the prosecutor and the defense.' She shook her head sadly. 'The defense was the worst. Fucking bastards made her out to be a teasing Lolita that deserved what she got.

'The jury found the man guilty and the judge sentenced him to five years probation. After a whole year dealing with the justice system and he got probation.' Her mouth opened and her voice cracked. 'She has to live with what he did the rest of her life and he gets…'

She glanced at the dirty looking man to see him staring out.

'You're aware of my price?' he asked.

'Yes. I managed to gather all of the money.'

'When I receive half I will do the job. When done I expect the other half.'

'I want you to make him suffer like my sister did. Can you do that?'

Purdy nodded.

'Who is this guy and where does he live?'

Purdy entered the library and sat at one of the computers. He searched Marcus Jenkins. Various New York newspapers ran stories on an underage girl assaulted in Greenwich Village. While the girl was walking home from a friend's house at 10 PM Marcus came up behind her and cracked the back of her head with a bottle. He then dragged her disorientated body down an alley and raped her. Jenkins was quickly found with the help of building cameras recording the street. Due to the head injury the girl sustained she wasn't able to identify Jenkins right away, a factor the defense tried to play up but failed to be successful.

Purdy had never researched up a victim before. Clients usually hired him to kill deadbeats who stole money from them or crossed them in some way. Greedy stupid people against greedy stupid people. This one was different. This one truly deserved to die for what he did. Ending his career on a good note seemed promising.

As soon as Purdy found the first half of the payment in his PO Box from Ms. Patel, he deposited it into his safety deposit and took the PATH into the city. His first stop was to a midtown sex shop on Broadway where he bought three large dildos made from soft, flexible material.

Further downtown he entered a hardware store where he purchased eight inch nails thick enough to pierce cement and clamps used to hold down large pieces of wood to a workbench for sawing.

Finally he stopped in a Wal-Mart to pick up bottles of ammonia, hydrogen peroxide, and lemon juice. Everything else he needed he had back at his apartment and could easily be disposed of after the job.

Dressed in a United States Post Office uniform, Purdy sat in the stolen car at the 23rd Street apartment building at Third Avenue and waited. The time was eleven thirty and the only people around the tree heavy block was an old man walking his dog and a couple of chatty college girls carrying portfolios and rushing to class at the art school down the street. Purdy exited the car, took the medium-sized box filled with all the items he needed out of the trunk, and walked to the apartment building.

In the vestibule he pressed the button for unit 2B.

'Yes?' a scratchy electrical voice asked.

'UPS. Package for Marcus Jenkins.'

The door buzzed and opened. Purdy climbed the steps to the second floor. Apartment 2B's door was ajar. He peeked inside.

'Mr. Jenkins?'

Purdy slipped inside and closed the door with his foot. He placed the box on the living room floor. He called out Jenkin's name again and said, 'I need you to sign for the package.'

A beeping went off from the kitchen down the hall.

Purdy removed his Maxim 9 from tablet pouch at his side and followed the sound. On the counter, a microwave finished its alarm. The coffee maker was on and sandwich sat on table. He bit his lower lip and listened carefully. Something blunt cracked across his skull. He blacked out before he hit the floor.

Purdy woke up on the floor in the living room. All his clothes were piled next to the open box. Laying on his front, his bare arms and ankles were hog-tied together behind him. Gray tape covered his mouth. Stretching his neck he spotted her sitting in the couch. Dressed for a day at the office, Ms. Patel had her legs crossed and a framed picture in her hand.

'You're up,' she said. 'It's about time.'

Purdy yelled obscenities through the tape. She smiled at his anger and flipped the picture over to reveal a medium shot of Ms. Patel and Raphael Durango at the beach. They wore swimsuits and held each other. Even though they wore sunglasses when they stared at each other their love was apparent. She tapped the frame with her wedding ring.

'I don't mean to be cliché, but do you get the picture?' she asked.

Purdy closed his eyes and tapped his head to the floor.

'I was very disappointed in Glossman's loyalty to you,' she said. 'Once I offered to let him go if he told me who killed Raphael, he gave me your name and location so quickly. At first I was worried that he was just giving me a name for the sake of his freedom. But I had no plan to let the man who ordered my husband's death go free. After a while I believed him. He had something truthful in his eyes. Or maybe it was the way he cried.'

She stood and walked around his body.

'So you know, the tools you gathered will make someone suffer.' She reached into the opened cardboard box and pulled out one of the dildos with nails angled through the sides and one spiked out the tip. 'Your work was for something.'

Purdy shook and slammed the floor. The bonds held tight around his limbs. The tape muffled his screams.

She frowned as tears threatened her eyes. She took a deep breath, held it, then released it.

'Let's get started.'

Purdy tensed up, closed his eyes, and imagined Mexico.

The Long Soak

Sandra Kohls

'Cut off her whit? No danger. Whit dae ye think ah am? Melba the fucking manicurist?'

'Her toes, ya muppet. You'd not be a manicurist – you'd be Pamela the pedicurist, no Melba the manicurist.'

'Whatever, man. There's no way ahm cutting aff anybody's toes, or any other body part for that matter.' Andy Cossar screwed up his face as a thought occurred to him. 'Anyway, is it no the fingerprints that are the problem? I've never heard of the Polis taking toeprints.'

Eddie Cossar shrugged. 'Aye, but it may have escaped your notice, she's no got any hands.'

They both looked down. If it wasn't for the fact that the water was scarlet and she was a corpse, she could've just been having a nice long soak after a hard day at the office. But it was true. There was a distinct lack of hands.

'Fuck's sake, man. Who would dae that to anyone?' Andy folded his arms and shook his head, as if he were looking at a bad plumbing job that he couldn't get the parts for.

'Some mad bastard.'

'Will we call the Polis, Eddie?'

'Oh aye.' Eddie minced picking up a phone

receiver and put on his best Kelvinside accent. 'Oh hello officer. Yes, this deid lassie just showed up in our bath. Yes, actually in the bath officer. God knows what that'll do to the enamel...' He shifted onto the other foot and swapped hands. 'What's that you say officer? My name? Eddie Cossar. Yes, that's right. That Eddie Cossar. My brother? Oh yes, He's here too. Certainly officer. We'll just get ourselves Bar-L body ready.' He glared at Andy. 'Toodle fucking pip. Officer.' He slammed down the imaginary phone. 'Are you mental?'

'But we didnae kill her.' Andy was attempting to pace the tiny room, a feat made challenging by his preferred diet of deep fried pizza suppers from Luigi's washed down with Yum Yums from Gregg's the bakers. Eddie wondered if there was a point where your stomach gave out and just exploded. If so, he hoped it didn't happen when he was around.

'Fuck's sake man. I know we didnae kill her. But what wi' us having an early bird reservation for many of Scotland's finest penitentiaries, Ah reckon the Polis might just no gie us the benefit of the doubt.'

'What are we going to do, then Eddie?'

Eddie sighed and took out his mobile. 'I'll phone big Johnny.' He said. 'He'll know how to sort it.'

Big Johnny's day hadn't started well. He'd spent the night having nightmares which involved being chased down a never ending spiral staircase by Sheriff

Woody & Buzz Lightyear, who had apparently gone rogue. Then he got up and stood on Grazer's tail, causing the wee shite to yowl like a banshee and run headfirst into the brand new standing mirror Elaine had bought last week, knocking it into the wall and leaving a dent in the recently applied 'peaceful eggshell' paintjob. What the fuck was a peaceful eggshell anyway? Then there had been nae milk for his coffee. Nae milk? What kind of housekeeper forgets milk? The dull buzz of his phone came from the pile of clothes he'd left lying on the bedroom chair last night. He answered it with a grunt. 'Aye?' He listened for a second, then rubbed a weary hand over his eyes. Clearly his day had started in the manner it meant to continue.

'Fuck's sake,' he hissed.

There was a high-pitched panicked screech coming out of the phone, and he held it away for a second, his face a resigned grimace.

'Don't move,' he said and hung up.

He padded downstairs, admiring, as he always did, the beautiful curve of the wide staircase. When he'd had the house built, that had been one of the features he'd insisted on. 'Sweeping, like.' He'd explained to the architect. 'Like in wan a they posh BBC dramas.' Elaine had added the chandelier. He'd not been too keen on that at first, especially when Scratcher Barr had called it 'a wee bit ponsey,' but now he could see that it gave the place an elegance which would have been lacking with your Ikea paper globe.

Elaine was sitting at the breakfast bar, elegantly puffing on a fag and dab-dabbing at her phone with expertly sculpted ice-blue fingernails. Johnny looked at her with satisfaction. Some of his pals' wives had let themselves go over the years, but not Elaine. She was still a cracker. A costly cracker, but one he didn't want to replace yet, despite the regular wee dalliances which he found himself partaking in from time to time.

'Alright doll?' Johnny poured himself an espresso and added a few sugar lumps. 'Has Mrs Lennox come back wi' the milk yet?'

Elaine nodded, her eyes still welded onto her phone. 'In the fridge.'

She tore her eyes away and smiled at him. 'Going out?' She took a last drag of her cigarette then bashed it into her empty espresso cup.

'Bit of business.'

'Haudit and Daudit giving you shite again?'

'How can you tell?'

'You always get a look. Like you've swallowed a hedgehog.'

'Aye well, they are a pair of pricks.' He scowled and downed his coffee then pulled on a pair of black leather gloves and a woolly bunnet. 'Right. See you later.' He aimed a peck at an expensively powdered cheek.

'Mmmm' said Elaine, engrossed again in the

bubbles being spewed up by Facebook messenger. 'Later.'

'A body in the bath?' Magic Malkie laughed as Johnny jumped into the plain white van parked at Cowcaddens. 'Marginally better than a horse's heid in the bed, eh? Who have those two eejits pissed off now?'

'Fuck knows.'

'Do they know who it is?'

'Some lassie. They don't recognize her. She's nae hands'

'Fuck's sake, man. That's harsh.'

'Aye.'

'Seriously Johnny, you need to get those two sorted.'

'Tell me about it.' Johnny said. 'Come on. Let's go.'

'Rubber ducks at your age?' asked Johnny marching into the bathroom. 'How many of the bastarding things do youse need?'

He stopped. 'Ah Fuck.'

She lay in the scarlet water. Her head faced the wall, and her blonde hair fell over her face and shoulders, streaks of bright red making it look like a really cheap dye job. The stumps of her arms were propped up on the bath rack. There was a tiny birthmark, the shape of Italy on her left shoulder.

'Dae ye recognize her, Johnny?'

Johnny took out his phone and walked out of the bathroom. Eddie and Andy looked at each other and shrugged, then followed him out.

'Aye, Johnny.' Andy's chins wibbled as he spoke. 'She was just lying there. Having a bath. Deid. Wi nae hands.'

Big Johnny finished his conversation and slipped his phone into his pocket then turned to Eddie.

'What have youse been up to?'

Eddie held his arms out in a silent shrug. 'Nothing Johnny, honest. We've no done nothing. Just the stuff you telt us tae do.'

'How do you know this lassie?'

'We dinnae,' Andy looked as if he was about to greet.

'Who the fuck have youse pissed aff?'

'Naebody, Johnny, honest. ' Eddie said.

'Naw, Johnny, honest. We wouldnae do that. Not after whit you said the last time.' Andy's big moon face looked sick.

Johnny rubbed his face. 'Jesus.' He paced to the window. 'Jesus,' he said again.

Johnny stared out the windows. What a view from this place. You could see the whole of Glasgow. Shame that it now belonged to two total bawheids. Their Da, his uncle Stuart, had been a smart man. Eddie and Andy though, had taken their share of genes from their mother, Gloria, a woman so glaiket you could hear the wind whistling in one ear and oot the other. Stuart's body had become unexpectedly acquainted with the pavement after either launching or being launched at it from a height of thirteen floors. Johnny had taken it as a warning shot and pulled back his quest for drug domination until he'd sorted the bastards he assumed had done it. Gloria had legged it as soon as the boys were old enough to be left, and was living with some small time crook near Penicuik. Was this another warning?

'Haw Johnny,' Andy said. 'Better no go tae the windae. Someone might see you.'

'Fuck's sake, Andy. We're on the thirteenth floor. They'd need tae have awfy long legs.'

Eddie silenced Andy with a glare. 'Sorry aboot him, Johnny. So what's the plan?'

Johnny looked at Magic Malkie. The man who made things disappear. He'd been standing silent, watching them as they were in the bathroom. At Johnny's look he nodded and slipped out the door.

Johnny headed towards the lounge, a man on a mission. He needed a whisky. Elaine was sitting on the sofa watching something on her laptop.

'What a day.'

Elaine turned her head towards him and smiled. 'Aye?' She was on the sofa, Grazer sprawled over her feet, tongue lolling.

He walked over to the bar and poured himself a

shot, then checked the ice bucket. 'Nae ice?'

'There'll be some in the freezer.'

'Fuck's sake. What do I pay that woman for?' He marched into the kitchen and flung open the freezer door. He stared for a moment then shut it. He opened it again. There, individually wrapped in cling film, the tips of the fingers poking out, lay two pale, well-manicured hands. It occurred to him that the nail varnish on these hands were a similar shade to the peaceful eggshell on their bedroom walls.

He picked one up and walked through to the lounge.

'Need a hand, doll?' Elaine picked up a glass of wine and took a delicate sip.

'What the actual fuck?' Johnny croaked, wielding the hand.

'Oh that.' She smiled.

'Jesus, Elaine, what have you done?'

'According to this,' Elaine nodded at the laptop screen, 'I've not done anything.'

Johnny hadn't noticed what she'd been watching when he'd come in, but now he saw himself displayed in full naked pixelated glory, dragging a body out of the bath and rolling it up in sheets of plastic, with the help of Andy and Eddie.

'Not the first time you've been naked with her, I imagine.'

Johnny walked over to the sofa and sat down. 'Jesus.' He rubbed his face and sat with his head in his hands for a couple of seconds. 'I wasnae sure. She looked different.'

'Being dead can do that to you. Did you not see the birthmark?'

'How did you do it?'

'Do what? Kill her, or set you up?'

'Both.'

'Well, I did have some help.' She smiled. 'Come on in,' she called in the direction of one of the arches leading off the lounge.

Johnny stared at the woman who strolled through the archway. She was fiftyish, dark haired and elegant. Nothing like the mousey wee woman she'd been the last time he'd seen her.

'Alright, Johnny?'

'Gloria.'

The woman glared at him. 'You're supposed to be keeping an eye on my boys, Johnny.'

'I never…'

'You promised me, Johnny. So how come they've been trying to muscle in on my man's territory?'

Ah fuck.

'What's the problem, Gloria? Does yer new man not want to help your boys?'

'Never mind him. It's me that doesn't want them around. Don't get me wrong. They're ma boys. But by God, Johnny...' She glowered at him. 'They're the way they are because of you and Stuart. Youse just kept pulling them in. From when they were wee boys.

They had no chance.'

'They had no brains,' Johnny muttered.

'Aye, well.' Gloria got up and helped herself to a whisky. 'Too bloody late, Johnny. You keep them away from me and on your patch, not ours. If they keep going the way they are, they'll get themselves killed.' She downed the whisky.

'I thought you didnae drink Gloria?'

'I've changed a lot since I got rid of that daft bastard I married.'

Johnny looked at her and shook his head. 'No way.'

'You'll never know, will you? But…,' she grinned, 'if you don't keep they boys away from me and out of trouble, someone will be getting an interesting present in their inbox.'

Johnny laughed. 'Aye, really? You know they'd be done too, if it ever came to it.'

'I don't care, Johnny. Better in jail than deid. Like your wee girlfriend.'

'She wasnae …'

'Ach come on Johnny. Do you think I button up the back?' Elaine stood up and came towards him.

'Come on, Doll.' Johnny tried to grab her hand. 'You know I'd never leave you.'

'Aye, now I do.' She poked him in the chest. 'I don't care what you do Johnny. You can have your wee bits of fun. But not with people I know.'

'You knew her?' Shit.

'She was my fucking beautician.'

Shit.

'I really liked her.' Elaine said, sniffing. 'Twice a week for the last five years she did my nails and my face and made me feel good. We got on. She was nice. And you had to go and shag her.'

'Sweetheart…'

'No.' She held a hand up. 'I've invested fifteen years into this marriage. I like my life. I even quite like you,' she paused, 'sometimes. So if you're thinking of replacing me…' She pointed to the laptop. 'This is my insurance. Oh, and we've more than one copy, so don't get any ideas.'

Johnny watched the two women pick up their handbags. 'We're going to the pub.' Elaine turned to look at him. 'You can keep the hands. A wee souvenir.'

'That went well.' Elaine picked up the bottle of Moët from the ice bucket and poured them both a glass.

'It did.' Gloria picked up her glass, then nodded at a dark, short-haired woman strolling over to their table. 'Better pour another.'

The woman smiled at them, sat down and lifted the glass. 'Ladies.' She knocked it back.

'God, you look totally different without your hair.' Elaine said, then grabbed her hands. 'And no nail varnish.'

'Just in case.' The woman poured herself another

glass. 'Did Malkie get the body back in time?'

'Aye.' Gloria nodded. 'Just had a text. Minus the hands, right enough, but who knows what goes on in these hospitals nowadays.' She laughed. 'Just cannae get the staff."

The woman's eyes widened. 'I can't believe how much like me she looked in the end. And with the hair extensions…'

'Took long enough to find her.' Elaine said. 'I was starting to think we'd never do it.'

The woman nodded.

'I'll miss you.' Elaine looked sad. 'What am I going to do on Tuesdays and Thursdays now? Who's going to do my nails and tell me the gossip?'

'You could always come visit us in Magaluf,' the woman said, looking hopeful. 'There's a new Beauty Salon opening, so I hear, thanks to a generous benefactor.'

They laughed.

'Well,' said Elaine, pouring them all a fresh glass. 'Here's to rubber ducks.'

They laughed again and raised their glasses. 'To rubber ducks,' they chorused.

Are Ye Askin'?

Mairi Murphy

Dreich and damp in the Barraland
Slipped into a pocket, ma weddin' band
Scarf pulled tight against the rain, seams straight
Queuin' up, coat wrapped round, worth the wait
Gettin' in, lipstick on, stand beside the wall
Scan the room, turn roon', answerin' the call
Of the first braw lad in a silver grey suit
Hair slicked, side shed, Chelsea boots
Askin' me up tae dance,
Ma china an' his pal, a wee romance
An' a lumber home, perchance tae roam
The dance flair

A waltz, a foxtrot, a modern twist:
Who knew livin' could be like this?
A chance meetin wi' Mr Right
On this wild November night
So clean cut he quotes the Bible
Wants hame early, he's entitled
Tae a bit kiss and cuddle in the close
So I'll go wae him, make the most
Of the weans bein' watched by ma' old man
The promise of a lift hame in his van
Shelter from sleet, the mist an' the rain
Avoidin' ma hellish life once again.

Bibliographies

Paul. D. Brazill

Paul D. Brazill's books include *The Last Laugh*, *Guns Of Brixton*, *Cold London Blues*, and *Kill Me Quick!* He was born in England and lives in Poland. His writing has been translated into Italian, Finnish, German, Polish and Slovene. He has had writing published in various magazines and anthologies, including *The Mammoth Books of Best British Crime*. His blog is at Pauldbrazill.com.

Natalie Crick

Natalie Crick, from Newcastle in the UK, has found delight in writing all of her life and first began writing when she was a very young girl. Her poetry is influenced by melancholic confessional Women's poetry. Her poetry has been published in a range of journals and magazines including *Cannons Mouth*, *Cyphers*, *Ariadne's Thread*, *Carillon* and *National Poetry Anthology 2013*.

Olga Dermott-Bond

Olga Dermott-Bond is originally from Northern Ireland, studied for an M.A. in English Literature at St Andrews University, and now lives in Warwickshire with her husband and two daughters. She was Warwick Poet Laureate in 2010, and has been commissioned to write for the *Poetry on Loan* scheme. Her poetry has been published in *The Canon's Mouth* and the online micropoetry broadside *Panning for Poems*. She teaches English and Drama, and enjoys all kinds of creative writing.

Georgi Gill

Georgi Gill is an Edinburgh-based poet who has been published in *Gutter*, *The Interpreter's House*, *Bare Fiction*, *Dactyl* and *Far Off Places*. Her poetry has also been included in *Signal*, a pamphlet of poems about the Leith Dazzle ship and the anthology, *A New Manchester Alphabet: An Illustrated Collection of New Poetry*. Most recently Georgi created the online *Mixed Messages* National Poetry Day project and was also guest editor for *The Interpreter's House* issue #63.

Michelle Ann King

Michelle Ann King was born in East London and now lives in Essex. Her stories have appeared in over seventy different venues, including *Interzone*, *Strange Horizons*, and *Black Static*. Her favourite author is Stephen King (sadly, no relation), and she also loves zombies, Las Vegas, and good Scotch whisky. She is currently working on her second short story collection — the first, *Transient Tales*, is available in ebook and paperback now from Amazon and other online retailers. See www.transientcactus.co.uk for full details and links.

Sandra Kohls

Sandra Kohls is a seasoned procrastinator, but still managed to graduate with merit from the University of Glasgow's Creative Writing Masters, as well as sneak her short stories and poetry into various anthologies. She is working on her first two novels, as being half German she is organised enough to neglect more than one book at a time. When she isn't working or writing, she goes running or swims up and down her local pool making up vengeful tales about people who do doggie paddle in the fast lane.

Tom Leins
Tom Leins is a disgraced ex-film critic from Paignton, UK. His short stories have been published by the likes of *Akashic Books*, *Shotgun Honey*, *Near to the Knuckle*, the *Flash Fiction Offensive* and *Spelk*. He is currently working on a novella called *Boneyard Dogs*. Get your pound of flesh at https://thingstodoindevonwhenyouredead.wordpress.com/

Cailean McBride
Cailean McBride has lived and worked Italy, Australia and in many places around the UK, primarily as a journalist. He lives in Scotland and is currently enrolled on the MFA programme in Creative Writing at the University of Glasgow.

Susan McLeod
Susan McLeod was born in Kilmarnock, Scotland and has worked in the pharmaceutical industry for 20 years. As part of her Creative Writing MA studies at Manchester Metropolitan University, she completed her first novel, *Pica* and is working on a sequel. Susan lives in Macclesfield.

David McVey
David McVey lectures in Communication at New College Lanarkshire. He has published over 100 short stories and a great deal of non-fiction that focuses on history and the outdoors. He enjoys hillwalking, visiting historic sites, reading, watching telly, and supporting his home-town football team, Kirkintilloch Rob Roy FC.

Christopher P Mooney
Glaswegian Christopher P. Mooney, who currently lives and works near London, writes crime fiction, horror fiction, adult fiction and eclectic poetry. His stories and poems have been published by *Spelk Fiction*, *Dead Guns Press*, *Devolution Z*, *Revolution John*, *Out of the Gutter*, *Yellow Mama*, *Horror-Sleaze-Trash*, *Romance Magazine* and *Open Pen*. His poem, *stark raving naked*, was the second-place prize-winner in *The Molotov Cocktail*'s inaugural Shadow Award poetry contest and was also a Sundress Press Best of the Net nominee. He is proud to have had a story in each of the first three editions of this publication. You can follow his creative efforts on Twitter - @ChrisPatMooney - and though his blog: https://playingwiththepoem.wordpress.com/ The story published here, *See No Evil*, was inspired by Fredric Brown's *Cry Silence*.

Mairi Murphy
Mairi has recently graduated with distinction from a Masters Course in Creative Writing from Glasgow University. She recently was awarded the Alistair Buchan Prize for poetry from the university for two of her poems and shortlisted for three. Published this year in *From Glasgow To Saturn* and *Shetland Create'* she is also featured in and the Editor of *Glasgow Women Poets* published by Four-em Press.

Kurt Newton
Kurt Newton's dark fiction and poetry has been published in a variety of places, in print and across internet, for more than twenty years now. His latest offerings can be found at *Zetetic: A Record of*

Unusual Inquiry, *Syntax & Salt*, and *Intrinsick*.

Maggie Powell
TV Extra and part-time Childminder Maggie Powell loves to write short form fiction. Her stories appear in women's magazines, anthologies and children's comics. Being part of Strathkelvin Writers gives Maggie plenty of inspiration and practice

M.E.Purfield
M.E. Purfield is the author of the *Miki Radicci* crime series, *Party Girl Crashes the Rapture*, and *Angel Spits*. You can find him at mepurfield.com

Steve Roy
Steve Roy lives in Atlanta and is an attorney by training, which some would say puts him squarely on the dark side itself, but at the very least, gives him an eye for darkness. He has always been fascinated with stories about the gray areas of good and evil and how they overlap in surprising ways. He has been writing for about eight years and has been published in numerous magazines and periodicals, as well as anthologies, such as Shadow Train, Red By Dawn and Deathlehem Revisited.

Lucy Rutherford
Lucy Rutherford lives in the City of Brighton and Hove – a never ending source of characters and inspiration. She has a Ph.D in criminology and published her first novel 'A Bunch of Lies' in 2016.Her second novel 'The Sun God's Daughter' is planned for release next year.

Anderson Ryle
Anderson Ryle is an engineer living in Fort Collins Colorado. He enjoys writing noir fiction, and has recently published his first noir short story *The Back Doors of Fancy Places*. He loves a good adventure, a dim jazz bar, and a smokey glass of single malt scotch.

Finola Scott
Finola Scott's poems and stories are widely published in anthologies and magazines including *The Ofi*, *Raum*, *Grind*, *Southlight*. She is proud to be a slam-winning granny. Currently she is mentored on the Clydebuilt Scheme by Liz Lochhead. When she's not on FB or writing, she enjoys chocolate, mahjong, Candy Crush Soda and her weer grand-girls, not necessarily in that order.

Angie Spoto
Angie Spoto is an American fiction writer and poet. She holds a dual-Bachelors degree in creative writing and business management from Lake Forest College and is completing a doctoral degree in creative writing at the University of Glasgow. She has lived in Austria, the Netherlands, and now lives in the UK. You can find more information about her publications on www.angiespoto.com.

Stephen Watt
Stephen Watt is a Glaswegian poet and the author of *Spit* and *Optograms*. He became the first crime poet to appear at Bloody Scotland during 2016, supporting Christopher Brookmyre and Mark Billingham. Appointed Dumbarton FC's Poet-in-Residence, Stephen's work has been published in several

countries while also making up one half of gothic spoken word and music duo Neon Poltergeist'

Jo Young

Jo Young is an Army veteran and mum to two young boys who, along with the dog, are her partners in crime and faithful Crooked Minions. She left the regular Army in 2014 and has been writing ever since. Her poetry has won prizes and appears in anthologies; her novels live in the knicker drawer. She is currently a doctoral student on the University of Glasgow's Creative Writing Programme.

Printed in Great Britain
by Amazon